ZOMBIES DON'T CRY

Borgo Press Fiction by BRIAN STABLEFORD

Alien Abduction: The Wiltshire Revelations
The Best of Both Worlds and Other Ambiguous Tales
Beyond the Colors of Darkness and Other Exotica
Changelings and Other Metaphoric Tales
Complications and Other Stories
The Cosmic Perspective and Other Black Comedies
The Cure for Love and Other Tales of the Biotech Revolution
The Dragon Man: A Novel of the Future
The Eleventh Hour
Firefly: A Novel of the Far Future
Les Fleurs du Mal: A Tale of the Biotech Revolution
The Gardens of Tantalus and Other Delusions
The Great Chain of Being and Other Tales of the Biotech Revolution
Halycon Drift (Hooded Swan #1)
The Haunted Bookshop and Other Apparitions
In the Flesh and Other Tales of the Biotech Revolution
The Innsmouth Heritage and Other Sequels
Kiss the Goat
Luscinia: A Romance of Nightingales and Roses
The Mad Trist: A Romance of Bibliomania
The Moment of Truth: A Novel of the Future
An Oasis of Horror: Decadent Tales and Contes Cruels
The Plurality of Worlds: A Sixteenth-Century Space Opera
Prelude to Eternity: A Romance of the First Time Machine
Promised Land (Hooded Swan #3)
The Quintessence of August: A Romance of Possession
The Return of the Djinn and Other Black Melodramas
Rhapsody in Black (Hooded Swan #2)
Salome and Other Decadent Fantasies
The Tree of Life and Other Tales of the Biotech Revolution
The Undead: A Tale of the Biotech Revolution
Valdemar's Daughter: A Romance of Mesmerism
The World Beyond: A Sequel to S. Fowler Wright's The World Below
Xeno's Paradox: A Tale of the Biotech Revolution
Zombies Don't Cry: A Tale of the Biotech Revolution

ZOMBIES DON'T CRY

A TALE OF THE BIOTECH REVOLUTION

BRIAN STABLEFORD

THE BORGO PRESS
MMXI

ZOMBIES DON'T CRY

Copyright © 2011 by Brian Stableford

FIRST EDITION

Published by Wildside Press LLC

www.wildsidebooks.com

DEDICATION

For Farah,

A True Inspiration

CONTENTS

CHAPTER ONE 9
CHAPTER TWO 21
CHAPTER THREE 31
CHAPTER FOUR .43
CHAPTER FIVE 57
CHAPTER SIX 69
CHAPTER SEVEN 81
CHAPTER EIGHT 93
CHAPTER NINE 105
CHAPTER TEN 115
CHAPTER ELEVEN 127
CHAPTER TWELVE 139
CHAPTER THIRTEEN 151
EPILOGUE 161
ABOUT THE AUTHOR 169

CHAPTER ONE

"Dying is easy," some great tragedian is supposed to have said, "comedy is hard." He was right, even though he didn't really know what he was talking about. I do. You can die in your sleep—in fact, it's hard to do it any other way—but you soon realize how difficult it is to raise a laugh when you're a zombie. All the jokes that would have gone down like a house on fire while you were alive fall flat. Nobody knows any longer how to respond to them. Nobody knows any longer how to respond to you—except, of course, for the fearful and the hateful, who pretend that life and afterlife and simple, even though they aren't.

In time, I guess, people will get used to it. Zombies will become familiar, if not exactly normal; it surely won't be long before we're given the right to vote, and offer ourselves as candidates for election. We're not short of clamoring voices, on-line if not in Parliament Square. The Knights of the Round Table were parochial plodders by comparison with the Knights of the Living Dead, and they only had an imaginary cup to chase and a few damsels in distress to protect, while we have our civil rights to pursue…and, alas, still a few damsels in distress to protect.

If only I hadn't died so young, I might have come back into a more hospitable world—but then, if I hadn't died so young, I wouldn't have afterlived through such interesting times, and might not have cared so much. I might even have been properly prepared for my afterlife, having given the possibility long and mature consideration in advance. Perhaps I should have done that anyway—nowadays, I reckon, everybody should—but I hadn't. I wasn't prepared, in any way whatsoever. It wasn't that I had thought, in life, that I had some kind of guarantee of protection from premature death—nobody's that stupid—but simply that I had more important things to think about, like scoring goals and sex.... I mean, being in love...and even, when I got really desperate, work.

Even if I had thought about it, though, I still wouldn't have thought it probable that I would die while I was still three years short of my thirtieth birthday—at which time the first zombies every created were still a decade shy of their thirtieth rebirthdays—simply because it wasn't. Sometimes, though, improbable things do happen. In fact, viewed with a cold objective eye, practically everything that happens is improbable—it's just that *something* has to happen (although nobody is entirely sure why), and, for that reason, something always has to be falling out of the vast chaos of improbable possibilities to become hard reality.

When you look at it that way, not only is everything improbable, but absurd. You couldn't make it up, as they say. People try, of course, but their fictions never quite match the perfect absurdity of actuality—there's always too much temptation to make things orderly, or ironic, or even to contrive happy endings. I know that because I have a degree in English Literature—or had, when I was alive

I've become much more of a philosopher than a reader since I became a zombie. Most of us do, although it's not what anyone would have expected in the days before Resurrection Technics existed, when the living only had the media image of "zombies" to go on.

The expectations of the living and the afterliving alike are almost always misled, but there's some comfort in the fact that the principle applies to our most nightmarish fears as well as our Utopian hopes.

The earliest zombies, whose rebirthdays—in 2025 or thereabouts—were about seventeen years in advance of mine, were only the prototypes, of course: duly certified freaks that everybody saw on TV and nobody expected to see at the bus stop or in the supermarket. When I became a zombie, therefore, it had only been seven years or thereabouts since the first zombies had, so to speak, been released into the wild. By the time I got into the act, it was no longer new, exactly, but it certainly hadn't gotten old yet. Nobody—and I mean *nobody*—knew as yet how to react to us, and we didn't know how to react to them. It was a learning process for everyone, and the whole absurd mess of pottage was still seething in the social cauldron.

The demand for the Resurrection Process to be licensed as a routine medical treatment had mostly come from the grieving and the *angst*-ridden, and it's arguable that the political sop in question might not have been offered in a time of economic well-being, rather than an era in which western capitalism was forty years past its use-by date, twenty years into the Second Great Depression, and only being sustained by a fear of the unknown that was way past rational terror and far into pathological territory—but I'll leave that discussion to the historians of the future. From my own viewpoint, the essential fact was that there had only been zombies abroad in England's no-longer-green-and-pleasant land for about as long as I had been gainfully employed, after leaving university with the customary massive debt. Most people I had known in life, including me, would still either look the other way or point them out as marvels if they saw a couple walking by. I say "a couple" because the vast majority felt safer traveling in pairs, even though it really wouldn't have made any difference at all if a mob had turned on them.

By and large, mobs didn't. Seeing zombies walking abroad was still too strange. Even mobs need tacit guidelines, and there simply wasn't anything in the reactive sector of the British collective unconscious to tell people what the "appropriate" response to real zombies was. Everybody had seen torch-wielding mobs hunting down Frankenstein's monster in old black-and-white movies, but if any substantial number of people had ever absorbed that into their twentieth-century instincts, they'd also had the absorption dissolved and leached away by the turn of the millennium, thanks to a hundred knowing repetitions in vivid color that had played the same scene as tragedy or farce. By 2020, even mythical flesh-eating zombies were allowed to figure in cheery slapstick comedies and cheesy romcoms...which is, I guess, another reason why it's now so hard for real zombies to raise a laugh, whether as jesters, stand-ups or Wildean wits.

But let's get on with the story....

* * * * * * *

At first, of course, I had no idea that I was a zombie. Nobody thought that it was a good idea to hand me a mirror when I first woke up, and my hands were still bandaged. It didn't strike me as particularly unusual that so many doctors were fussing over me when I first came round. One of the juniors told me, when I was eventually able to ask the question, that I'd been caught in the blast of an ED suicide bomb, but he didn't bother to add that my injuries had been fatal.

Perhaps he thought he was protecting me. Perhaps he thought that it wasn't the kind of news that he, as a living person, ought to be responsible for delivering.

It didn't strike me as strange, either, that I had a zombie nurse. Like everyone with nothing better to do, I watched *Resurrection Ward* on BBC-1 every Sunday evening, right after *Songs of Praise*. I even watched it if I happened to be on my own in the flat, although it was much better watching it with Helena, at her place or mine, so that we could laugh together at its not-quite-absurdity, and occasionally get misty-eyed at its pretty triumphs and tragedies.

The show had been running for three years by June 2042, so no matter how bizarre people might have thought it if they'd run into a zombie estate agent or a zombie fire-fighter, nobody found anything particularly bizarre in the notion of a zombie nurse. It didn't even strike me as strange that the zombie nurse seemed to be in sole charge of checking my monitors, changing my drip and replacing my urine-bag.

I had to be told before I was allowed any visitors, though.

The zombie nurse's name-badge identified her as "Pearl"—no surname. When she got around to telling me that I'd "passed on," while she was peeling off the dressings to reveal my white hands—which might not have triggered any alarm bells, given that I wouldn't have expected them to look entirely normal—she looked at me with a hint of trepidation as well as just a soupçon of compassion in her pink eyes. She didn't curl her lip at the euphemism, though, and she didn't manifest the slightest vestige of a tear. Zombies don't.

Would I have burst into tears if I'd still been able to? Perhaps—but I doubt it. In a soap opera, the revelation wouldn't have qualified as a poignant moment.

When you think about it, an inability to shed tears doesn't really qualify as an inconvenience. It would if it meant that the conjunctiva dried out completely, but zombie tear-ducts do produce enough moisture to keep the eyeball lubricated; they just don't produce the superabundant moisture that makes you *blub*. They don't produce "emotional tears." The only people who cry when they watch a particularly poignant episode of *Resurrection Ward* are the living.

As the news that I was a zombie sank in, therefore, I simply looked at the dry-eyed zombie nurse with dry eyes of my own—by no means beginning to bond, as yet, but at least offering a symbolic gesture toward the bonding that might be to come.

Then I looked at the sick-but-living people in the other beds. None of them was looking at me. They were all older than me, most of them much older. Most of them were more conscious—it was early afternoon—but none of them was looking at me, at that particular moment. That wouldn't have seemed significant before, but now that I knew, it did.

"I'm not on the Resurrection Ward," I said to the nurse, in an exceedingly reasonable tone. "If I were a zombie, surely I'd be on the Resurrection Ward."

Nurse Pearl didn't frown at my use of the term *zombie*. "We don't have a Resurrection Ward, as such," she told me. "That's just a TV show. Maybe they have them in the big London hospitals, but this is the Royal Berks, and anyone our doctors can bring back from the dead gets a bed wherever we can free one up, just like everyone else."

Then I asked for a mirror. She had one ready.

I didn't recognize myself, and not just because my once-brown hair was beginning to grow back the color of snow, or because my once-blue eyes were now pink. I'd always been a trifle pale—pale enough to be called "zombie" in jest on occasion, especially by my team-mates and opponents in the Sunday Morning League, although it had never reached the pervasiveness of a nickname—so my complexion wasn't so very different. The shape of my features had changed, subtly but unmistakably.

"I thought the whole point of using superstimulant stem-cells regenerated from the patient's own body for the purposes of resurrection was to restore appearance, even to people whose faces got blown off in a bomb-blast," I said, still proud of my level tone.

"It's not as simple as that," she told me.

I knew that, really. *Inside*, I still felt like me, but I knew that it wasn't as simple as that. I knew that nothing, from now on, was ever going to be as simple as "that" again.

But I did feel like *me*, inside. I still felt as if that, at least, was simple. Everything might have changed, but something still seemed to be the same, however paradoxical that might be in logical rather than emotional terms.

I took a closer look at Nurse Pearl then. *Resurrection Ward* had made the sight of zombies in nurses' uniforms familiar, but familiarity is in the eye of the beholder, and I was a different beholder now that I'd seen my own pink eyes. I could no longer take my zombie nurse for granted, now that I'd realized why she'd been assigned primary responsibility for my care.

Pearl wasn't as pretty as the actresses who played nurses in the soap, in wigs and pancake make-up, but she *was* young—no older than me, I guessed. I was already aware, vaguely, that zombies in their twenties were relatively rare, for simple reasons of demographic probability, but the relevance of the datum now seemed suddenly acute.

"Traffic accident or bomb-blast?" I asked her, knowing that my gaze would fill in the context.

"Neither," she said, bluntly. "I committed suicide."

I had also been aware, in the vague sense that one knows all sorts of irrelevant details, that the physicians carrying out resurrections were supposedly forbidden to discriminate, ethically obliged to make such attempts on any and all suitable corpses—as well as quite a few unsuitable ones, in order to be on the safe side—and *Resurrection Ward* had tackled the seeming paradoxicality of resurrecting suicides on more than one occasion, but that hadn't prepared me to respond to the conversational gambit in question. I didn't know what to say. My gaze presumably asked *why*, but she wasn't in a mood to answer questions that hadn't been voiced, and would probably have told me that it was none of my business if it had.

"I suppose most of your zombie patients are older than me," was what I finally contrived to say instead.

"Twenty-somethings are in a small minority in the afterliving community, it's true," she admitted. She still didn't frown at the term I'd used, but she put a slight emphasis on her substitute. It occurred to me that she was probably following some kind of standard script that she'd had to memorize during retraining, like any other civil servant. "The old outnumber the young even among the living nowadays," she continued, "but the disproportion between those who die old and those who die young is dramatically exaggerated among the afterliving. Afterliving individuals who died in their twenties comprise a small minority within a tiny one—unless you take sides with those who think that age of death is irrelevant to the afterliving, and that only the duration of afterlife counts. On that basis, none of the regulars at the Center is more than seven years old—which probably explains why they tend to behave like a gang of naughty kids."

"The Center?" I queried.

"The local Afterlife Center, aka Zombie Rehab, aka the old Salvation Army Hall on Mount Pleasant. You'll be spending a lot of time there soon enough. So do I, shifts permitting." She didn't frown at her own use of the word *zombie* either.

Stupidly, I could only remember lines from *Resurrection Ward*, spoken in similar situations—but I wanted to script my own. After a pause, I came up with: "Let's hope we really can live forever, then—that way, we'll live to see the day when the dead outnumber the living, and the duration of our afterlives will have so far outstripped the time before our deaths that we'll have forgotten we were ever alive."

She didn't laugh—but that was okay, because I wasn't sure that it had been a joke.

"It might be best to concentrate on living one day at a time, for now," she said, "and leave the far future to take care of itself." That didn't sound as if it had come from a script cooked up by a committee but it didn't exactly sound as if it came from the heart either. In fact, her voice had taken on a distinct sarcastic inflection, which sounded as if it was more natural to her than the insipid tone she'd been trying to maintain thus far.

"I don't feel any different," I told her, emphatically. If *Resurrection Ward* had a message, or even a gist, it was the insistence that an afterliving person isn't the same person as the living person he or she had been before—that rebirth isn't really *re*birth at all, but the beginning of something new. I'd been told more than once by artfully-resentful zombies, however, that all of that was just propaganda invented by the living as an excuse for depriving the afterliving of the property, social status and human rights they'd enjoyed in life. As with the weeping thing, I hadn't really cared much one way or another, and the script I was obliged to follow on behalf of the Ombudsman's Office wouldn't have allowed me to express any sympathy if I'd felt any.

Now, I cared. Now, I wanted an expression of sympathy,

whether it was in Nurse Pearl's professional script or her sarcastic nature or not. It probably was in the script, but Nurse Pearl was presumably something of a natural rebel.

"It doesn't matter what you feel right now," she assured me, brutally. "You'll get the hang of being different soon enough. The people you knew and loved will help you with that, if not much else."

It wasn't her embittered tone that struck me so much as her use of the past tense; People I *knew* and *loved*.

But I still love them, I thought. *Mum, Dad, Kirsten...Helena. Surely they'll still love me, zombie or not. They aren't bigots.*

What I said aloud, warily, was: "What do you mean, *not much else?*"

"Sorry," she said. "I'm not supposed to do that—not according to the retraining manual. Just because we've got pink eyes, though, it doesn't mean we have to rose-tint the world. I've seen your family, mind—your mother, your father, your sister. They've all put in their stints of duty while you were in the post-mortem coma. They seem nice. Maybe they'll let you down gently, if at all."

"Yours didn't?" I asked. It wasn't the first question that sprang to mind, but it seemed the most polite.

"Well," she said, "I did kill myself. They were bound to take it personally, I guess."

"But you're okay now?" I asked, solicitously. "You're not about to do it again?"

"Technically," she told me, "I can't. I'm already dead, so I can't kill myself. Nobody's contrived to put a word in the dictionary, as yet, for what zombies do instead, in spite of the... incidents. None of the improvised suggestions has caught on to the extent of becoming common parlance."

I didn't needed to ask what the "...incidents" were. Whatever zombies did instead of "killing" themselves had been featured on *Resurrection Ward* too. I was beginning to regret not having been a more assiduous viewer; I had a feeling that I might have need of every last drop of the show's educational value, even if it was set in a place that didn't really exist, at least in the Royal Berkshire Hospital.

"What about Helena?" I said. "You've seen her too, I assume."

Nurse Pearl hesitated.

"She's my girl-friend," I said, emphasizing the present tense ever so slightly.

"I've seen her," the zombie nurse admitted.

"She *has* visited—while I was…pupating." I wasn't entirely sure of the jargon, but I was fairly sure that the afterliving liked to refer to the post-mortem coma as "pupation," thus implying, if only in jest, that their new status was analogous to that of a butterfly, whose previous existence had been merely larval.

"Yes," said Nurse Pearl. "She did visit." Past tense again.

"And she'll be back, as soon as she hears that I'm awake," I said. "When's visiting time?"

"The doctors haven't given the go-ahead yet," she told me. "The Burkers will probably want to do a few more tests—and then there's the psych evaluation. Tomorrow, maybe."

"Burkers?" I queried, having misheard it as *burkas*.

"Bad joke," she said. "Burkers as in Burke and Hare. Resurrection Men. Popular slang two hundred years ago, now back in fashion, in certain circles, with the irony reversed. Who says the afterliving have no sense of humor, eh?"

I didn't laugh. "How long will the tests take?" I asked.

"A couple of hours, maybe—longer if your nerves and muscles aren't playing ball. Same with the psych evaluation—an hour or so if you get the answers right…no limit if you screw it up."

I'd seen psych evaluations for the risen dead on *Resurrection Ward* too, and had run the gauntlet of those designed for the living on more than one occasion. I had no fear of them. I'd never felt saner in my life…although, even as I formulated that thought, I realized that it was the kind of observation that might be open to misinterpretation, given my present circumstances.

"Can I have my phone?" I asked. "Or was it a casualty of the bomb-blast?"

"Even if it hadn't been, you wouldn't have been able to use it," she said. Her voice was back in neutral.

"Can I borrow a laptop, then? I need to do some research on the web." Actually, I wanted to check my email. I didn't know how long I'd been out, but I figured that it must really be piled up.

"Not yet," she said.

And then—just like that—she was called away, to attend to the needs of a living patient.

I looked around again. Nobody was looking in my direction. Suddenly, as the only person on the ward who was—as yet—in the ranks of the afterliving, I felt very much alone.

CHAPTER TWO

I suppose that I had had more forewarning of what it might be like to join the ranks of the afterliving than anyone else in Reading, except for medical professionals, even if I hadn't taken full advantage of the forewarning in question. As a caseworker in the Ombudsman's Office, I had seen far more of the afterliving when I was alive than most living individuals, and had certainly had far more one-to-one conversations with them than even medical professionals generally contrived, or bothered, to have. It's not difficult to conceive a sense of grievance when you're a zombie, and the OO is the dustbin of English desperation, where appeals against injustice go to die, never to rise again. I'd been very well aware of the absurdity of the whole bureaucratic process even before I died myself—to the extent that I knew there would be no point going to the OO as a zombie client.

Having worked for the OO, I already knew how vanishingly unlikely it was that I'd get my old job back, however unfair that unlikelihood might be. Parliament had been quick to license resurrection as a medical procedure, for reasons of political expediency, but it was being vey slow indeed—for similar reasons of political expediency—to follow up its instant creation of a new category of citizens with the corollary legislation that would give them the same rights as everyone else.

To put it bluntly, it wasn't illegal, in 2042, to discriminate against the dead, even if they were just as capable of doing their old jobs as they had been when they were alive. Given that unemployment among the living was running at almost twenty-five per cent, even in Reading, it wasn't entirely surprising that unemployment among the afterliving should be running at more than ninety per cent.

The law will catch up with our formal entitlements in the end, I suppose—though maybe not in a standard lifetime. Justice is another matter; if I were a cynic—and I never met a zombie who wasn't—I'd probably argue that there never had been any and never would be. Thanks to the wonders of biotech, unicorns and flying pigs are even more commonplace nowadays than zombies, but justice? That really is incredible.

I'd been told more than once while on duty in the offices of the OO, by zombies who were taking the art of grievance to a new level, that the reason zombies can't manufacture melanin, and are therefore albinos, is that the Resurrection Men planned it that way, as a deliberate biotech plot intended to mark them out and prevent them from passing for the living, thus making it far easier for everyone else to discriminate against them.

I'd also been told more than once, by Englishmen of Pakistani or Jamaican or Somali or Turkish or Indonesian or Nepalese descent—all the other people, in fact, that England's so-called Defenders were trying to defend their mythical England against—that the reason the Resurrection Men had elected to make zombies whiter than white was to make even easier to discriminate against people of color. Some people seemed genuinely to believe that the greatest biotech miracle of the twenty-first century had been cooked up, in its entirety, simply to give existing "white" people an opportunity to claim that that people of color had no right to complain about discrimination, since people devoid of color had it even worse than they did. That belief, of course, didn't stop them complaining that the Resurrection Men were also discriminating against them by favoring "white" people for resurrection—in spite of the fact that devout Muslims and Afro-Anglicans were the loudest advocates of the thesis that the afterliving were actually demons sent to plague the living by Satan or Iblis, and that God-fearing people should *never* sign consent forms licensing the use of resurrection technology on their loved ones.

I'd been cynical enough, even as a living person, to think that all of those arguments, except the most blatantly paradoxical and hypocritical, might have a seed of truth within them. I had, however, been quite content to take refuge in the standard script supplied for my use by the Ombudsman's Office, which required me to point out that there were other physiological distinctions between the living and the afterliving that science had yet to explain, and that none of those were the kind of device that might have been planned for the purposes of stigmatization, so that the albinism of the afterliving was almost certainly an accident of physiological happenstance rather than any kind of cunning conspiracy.

I still believed that when I woke up to the afterlife myself, partly because it still seemed convincing, and partly because I didn't want to think that the Royal Berks Burkers were anything but angels of mercy, who, having regrettably failed to save my life, had done the next best thing.

* * * * * * *

By the time I got a chance to have another chat with Nurse Pearl, the first afternoon of my afterlife was wearing on and I was already bored out of my skull. The other patients in the ward were beginning to take notice of me, though—at least, the guy who put his stiffened index-fingers together in the shape of a cross when I tried to get out of bed condescended to notice me.

He made the same sign of the cross whenever Pearl strayed too close to his bed, although she always left it to the other nurses on the ward actually to attend to his needs. Evidently, patients were allowed to exercise their rights of choice in matters of care, if not in the matter of who got the next bed.

I assumed that the patient with the busy index-fingers wasn't *really* trying to ward off demons, and that the gesture was more joke than insult. He was probably bored out of his skull too, and desperate for any distraction he could improvise. If I'd been able to do it, I'd have gone over to his bed, wiggled my fingers at him and moaned "woo-oo-oo" just to play my allotted part in the comedy, but I was still attached to the catheter as well as the drip; standing up was pretty much out of the question, let alone walking around. I don't suppose he'd have laughed, though, any more than he'd have expired in mortal terror.

Nurse Pearl didn't bother to ask me how I was feeling when she was finally able to get back to me, but she had the grace not to make a show of being bored while she answered questions she must have been asked a dozen times before. It was her job to answer them, as best she could, but it was also her responsibility as one afterliving individual to another, and she took that seriously.

"Just give me a few tips," I said, trying not to sound as if I were pleading. "The things to watch out for that only fellow zombies know...you know what I mean."

"Not really," she lied, perhaps diplomatically. "The afterliving aren't all alike, any more than the living are. One zombie's meat is another man's brain, as they say, inaccurately and in really bad taste."

I didn't laugh at the appalling joke, but that was because it was so appalling, not because I'd lost my sense of humor.

She hastened to add: "On which subject, you might find that your appetites are a trifle peculiar. I'm assured that the cravings are no odder, and no worse, than the ones living women routinely get when they're pregnant, but I wouldn't know. Our dietary requirements are supposedly slightly different, although the physiologists haven't worked out exactly how yet, let alone why. *Don't worry about it* is the only real advice I can give you on that score. You'll work out your likes and dislikes in time."

"Okay," I said. "What else? Be careful of direct sunlight, of course—I know that one."

"Right. Most indoor light won't hurt your eyes or skin, but you might have to be careful if we get a sunny day tomorrow—daylight can be fierce, even though window-glass. When you get out, you'll have to be *very* careful, even if you only have go out in order to get back and forth from the Center. It's June, unfortunately, and the sun is higher in the sky than at any other time of the year. It might not feel hot, but the danger of burning is very real. You'll be given factor-32 sun cream when you're discharged, and a repeat prescription for more. Use it religiously."

"Right," I said, hoping that I'd remember.

"When the sedation wears off, you'll almost certainly get restless leg syndrome and various prickling sensations—but all that will fade once you start on physiotherapy at the Center. To be perfectly honest, calling it *physiotherapy* is distinctly overgenerous, but it *is* exercise, and it will get you fit. Stan runs the Center, so we have to put up with his little idiosyncrasies. You'll find out what I mean soon enough. Apart from that…you might as well take things as they come, because there's really not much I can do to prepare you for it."

"I'll still be able to play football, won't I? I mean…obviously, I'll still be *able*…but I won't have lost my skills?"

"Probably not," she said, with what seemed to be undue wariness. "But that doesn't mean that you'll be able to get a game. What kind of football did you play?" Past tense again.

"Real football—soccer. Does it make a difference?"

"Not in practical terms—I only asked because we have an ex-rugby player at the Center. Bad tackle caused a cerebral haemorrhage. I thought you might have something useful in common. He's the next youngest, in terms of death date, after you and me, at least until…." She changed the subject abruptly: "I'll bring you a laptop once the consultant gives me the thumbs up—then you can do your own research—but you'd be wise not to believe all you read. And if you're hoping to catch up with your email, forget it. Your account will have been cancelled. You password won't work."

That hadn't occurred to me. It was the first practical reminder that feeling like myself wasn't sufficient to being myself. No matter how similar to the old me the new me turned out to be, the old me was still legally dead. All my socioeconomic contracts would have to be remade...if possible.

I still had the mirror that Pearl had given me earlier. I'd been looking into it at intervals for hours. I took yet another peep. "Can't complain, I suppose," I said. "I was no oil painting before. My facial hair will still grow, won't it?" I wasn't absolutely certain about that, because my face looked uncannily smooth from where I was propped up on my pillows.

"Yes," she confirmed, "your hair will grow, on your chin as well as your head. It will probably be markedly different in texture, though—softer and silkier. I gave you a depilatory this morning, before you woke up. You won't need another for several days—maybe a week."

"Thanks," I said, absent-mindedly. "Could you possibly let Helena in to see me before tomorrow, if she comes, or are you absolutely committed to following doctor's orders?"

"Absolutely committed," she told me.

It didn't seem to be an appropriate time for making jokes about the legendary slavishness of zombies, so I didn't attempt one.

"Do you know how many other people were killed in the bomb blast that took me out?" I asked, after a slight pause.

"Seven," she told me. "Thirty-four injured, not counting trivial cuts and bruises. The worst one ever in Reading, and the worst ever credited to England's Defenders, although there've been higher casualty-counts in Slough and London, courtesy of jihadists. I was on duty when the victims began to come in—I don't usually work A and E, but it was all hands on deck that day. It caused some problems for the patients already in care, but mercifully not enough to generate a morality-blip. The last thing you need after an incident like that is to trigger an automatic inquiry."

"And how many of the seven were zombifiable?" I asked, not having much interest in the intricacies of Hospital Trust computer monitoring.

"Five attempts were made, but you were the only one who

pulled through. The burns on your head, torso and arms were superficial—it was a single piece of flying glass that actually killed you, slicing cleanly through your heart and lung. The people who caught the nails that were packed around the plastic explosive weren't so lucky—their wounds were far messier."

"Lucky," I repeated, with no particular inflection.

"Very," she insisted.

Obviously she wasn't about to license any suspicion that being reincarnated as a zombie might be considered less than lucky. How could she? She'd thought being alive was so unlucky that she'd killed herself.

Maybe some day, I thought, being a zombie would seem the preferable option to all the living, and no one would even hang around long enough to breed, thus bringing the human story to a terminus of sorts. Zombies could enjoy sex—*Resurrection Ward* was very clear about that—but thus far, there was no known case of any female zombie falling pregnant. Nobody was yet prepared to declare it absolutely impossible, but nobody was yet prepared to rule it possible either.

I took the safer route in the discussion of luck. "Taking a piece of flying glass full in the chest has to be reckoned pretty unlucky, in my book," I observed. "One of those freaks of chance that make truth stranger than fiction. Being within the blast-radius of a suicide bomb in Berkshire was pretty unlucky, too, given that the newsblips keep telling us that we're still more likely to get struck by lightning, let alone drown in the bath. Where did the psychopathic idiot blow himself up, exactly? I've been thinking hard, but the last thing I can remember is going to the library in my lunch break to restock my e-reader."

"The ground floor of the Oracle, near the entrance to TK Maxx."

"I must have been taking a short cut back to the office. Why there? It's not exactly ghetto territory."

"I don't think he was trying to target the immigrant population as such, or even protesting specifically about demographic change in Reading. He was just making a point."

"The point in question being that the self-appointed defenders of mythical England are just as crazy as the self-appointed defenders of the mythical Prophet—that if Islam can produce suicide bombers by the score, the Bulldog Breed can't be found wanting in the fatal fanaticism department. At least there's no possible question of resurrecting suicide bombers…is there?"

"Not really," she admitted. "Even the ones who go off too soon and don't do much damage to others generally succeed in blowing their own brains to smithereens, so the question of moral entitlement doesn't arise there. The Jarndyce case was adjourned again while you were comatose, though. No one's entirely sure which way it will go."

Blaise Jarndyce was a paedophilic serial killer dying in Broadmoor of liver and pancreatic cancer. According to the newsblips, he was a goner—but once the tumors had been cleaned out of his dead body, he might be a candidate for resurrection, and the fact that zombies sometimes developed personalities totally different from those they'd had in life was likely to work in his favor. The case had already dragged on more than somewhat, and looked likely to run to run to epic lengths if stopgap measures were put in place when the evil sod actually kicked the bucket. No one knew how long a person might be able remain suspended in a post-mortem coma, neither dead nor afteralive.

"The stupid thing is," I said, "that the ED didn't have any reason to hate me before, given that I was born white, but now that, thanks to them, I'm whiter than white, they will hate me, because they don't like Olde English zombies any more than they like Englishmen of Jamaican or Pakistani descent. Ironic, eh?"

"Ironic," she confirmed, humourlessly. "I have to go now. I have other patients to attend to."

"Be thankful you've got a job," I said. "All the zombies I ever met were unemployed, and bitter about it. It wasn't a representative sample, mind—I worked for the OO." The past tense slipped out without my noticing it.

"There's actually a demand for zombie nurses," she told me. "*Resurrection Ward* has made sure of that, at least. I was unemployed *before*, but I was accepted for fast-track retraining with no trouble at all, and taken on at the Berks as soon as I finished. Ironic, eh?"

She turned to go, not waiting for the echo, but there was still one more question I needed to ask.

"It is okay, isn't it, for *us* to call ourselves and one another *zombies*? But not for *them*." The *them* slipped out too. I suppose I should have congratulated myself for the speed of my adaptation.

"It really doesn't matter," she told me. "We are what we are, and we have to find out what that is before we can get used to it. It doesn't matter what standards of political correctness the living invent, or how conscientiously or otherwise they observe them. Whether they call us *zombies* or the *afterliving*, we are what we are."

I wondered, briefly, how the other living patients in the ward—apart from the guy with the symbolically-inclined index-fingers—might be reacting secretly to being nursed by a zombie, but I figured that they would mostly be well aware that they ought to be grateful for any care at all. I wasn't so sure about the living who had been numbered among my own former clients, many of whom had been ED sympathizers or people the ED wanted rid of. In either case, they might well have felt a trifle uncomfortable at having their appeals against the perceived injustice fielded by a victim of collateral damage to an ED suicide-bomb.

That wasn't an irrelevant consideration, so far as I was concerned, even though my contract of employment had been voided by my death. In theory, there was nothing to stop me reapplying for my old job—or, of course, from taking the matter to the Ombudsman's Office if I were rejected, on the grounds of unfair discrimination. After all, I knew the drill as well as anyone.

I wasn't left alone with my thoughts for very long, though.

As Pearl had said, the doctors still had tests to do, and they were used to working unsocial hours.

CHAPTER THREE

The question most frequently asked about the afterliving is whether zombies still suffer from *angst*, and, if so, how their *angst* differs from the *angst* of the living. Well, not really—only joking. In an ideal world, though—meaning one in which people took existentialist philosophy as seriously as it deserves to be taken—that would probably be *one* of the most frequently-asked questions.

Naturally, I've developed my own approach to the question.

I contracted myopia in infancy, when I was alive. It was corrected by laser surgery as soon as it was diagnosed, but it's difficult for adults to figure out that a kid's vision is blurred and difficult to measure the extent of the blurring, until he's learned to recognize the letters of the alphabet, because that's what standard eye-tests involve, so it wasn't until I was five that I was diagnosed. One of the side-effects of infantile myopia—which can't be corrected by subsequent surgery—is that the blind spots around the junctions of the optic nerve and the retina increase in size in the still-developing eyes. The fact that eyes have blind spots doesn't make all that much difference to normal vision, because a pair of eyes can get enough information between them not to miss objects in the environment. If you close one eye, though, small objects at which you look directly do tend to disappear from view—and that phenomenon is much more marked in the once-myopic. The odd thing is, however, that you're not conscious of any gap in the field of vision; you can only become aware of the disappearance if you rotate your head from side to side, so that the object alternates between visibility and invisibility. It's not that the brain fills in the gap but rather that it refuses to register the fact that there *is* a gap.

When my afterlife began, I assumed that the situation would be similar with respect to zombie consciousness. Like the once-myopic, I figured, the once-living simply wouldn't notice the voids where fragments of their former selves had gone missing. That made me suspicious of myself, and suspicious of my sensation of being the same self as I'd ever been. So yes, in a word, the afterliving *do* suffer from *angst*—a cognitively fundamental fear of death—even though the prospect of death is behind them instead of in front of them. They suffer from an inherent fear of what Death the Sneak-Thief might have done to them.

As for a counterpart to *angst*, which hasn't yet been definitively named, any more than what the afterliving do instead of dying…well, I guess we have that too, even though the as-yet-unconfirmed possibility exists that, barring accidents and acts of extreme violence, afterlife might last forever.

So, even though I didn't feel any different from the way I'd felt when I was alive, I did stop taking myself quite so much for granted, even while I was still in hospital. Although I seemed to myself to be exactly the same person I'd been before, I was careful, from the very beginning, as any conscientious ex-myopic individual would be, to remind myself continually that I'd probably feel like that even if I wasn't the same person, because my brain would simply ignore the gaps where the aspects of the old me had been that weren't there any more.

What I didn't doubt, however, was that the bits of the old me that *were* still there were still the same. I was convinced that I'd still be able to play football like a Sunday morning maestro, no matter how difficult it might be to get a game, and I was absolutely certain that I was still in love, with Helena. And that, I thought, was the most important thing of all.

Was I a fool? I don't think so.

The real situation, I must admit, isn't quite as simple as my myopia analogy implies. The afterliving individuals whose brains need to be restored by the all-conquering superstimulant stem-cells don't just have "gaps" where they were patched up, because the neuroarchitecture of the brain does far more than store memories. Zombies don't just have issues with forgetfulness, but with the dispositions of their personality. Indeed—although it might, of course, be mere propaganda invented by the living to justify stripping the afterliving of their property, their social status and their human rights—it seems to be an arguable case that "passing on" invariably and necessarily involves alterations in that sort of disposition. But continuity survives, even so. The once-myopic eye can still see, and the once-living mind can still understand. We might be different people, but we're also the same.

Zombies don't cry, and nobody laughs at their jokes, but zombies *can* still love the people they loved in life, and can still be *in love* with the people they were in love with in life and nobody—not even the most skeptical philosopher in the world—is entitled to doubt that, or reckon it less than a tragedy if that love becomes suddenly unrequited.

* * * * * * *

Mercifully, there wasn't a great deal of poking and prodding while the Mighty Burkers of the Royal Berks examined their handiwork and pronounced it good. There were no jabbing needles at all, except for the drip that was still attached to my arm, even though I was no longer *nil by mouth*. They even took the catheter away, eventually.

Mostly, they wanted to see what I could do on my own; they tested the wiggle in all my fingers and toes, and gradually moved from the extremities inwards, checking sensation and co-ordination. They tested my hearing, my speech and my eyesight as well as my sense of touch, and even did a sniff test of sorts to ascertain whether my sense of smell could still recognize such crude indicators as amyl acetate and Jeyes fluid. They weren't big on answering questions, though. While the tests were in progress, the Mighty Burkers were way too busy, and when the tests were concluded, they were in way too much of a hurry. They had other dead people to resurrect, other minds to remodel, other albinos to throw on the dole.

When they addressed me at all, they called me "Mr. Rosewell" or "Nicholas," as if to emphasize that I was a new man. I didn't bother to tell them that my friends called me Nicky. After all, I thought, if there was ever a good opportunity to seize the reins of my own destiny and renickname myself "Nick," this was it.

Did I want to take it, though?

I wasn't sure—but for the time being, I thought, I'd let my friends continue calling me Nicky, for old time's sake, and I decided that I'd *always* be Nicky to Helena…and I'd let the Resurrection Men continue calling me "Mr. Rosewell," or "Nicholas."

"Must be stressful coping with the extra work-load," I said to one harassed junior who lingered longer than most. He wasn't wearing a name-badge but had introduced himself, in a mutter, as Dr. Hazelhurst. "You probably had enough work when you only had to cope with the living, without having to tend the needs of the afterliving as well."

"Actually," he told me, "it's far from being a nuisance. Afterlife medicine is the hot specialism right now—other areas of expertise haven't exactly run out of ignorance, but it's hard to make any sort of major breakthrough on such well-trodden ground. Afterlife is wide open, saturated with unknowns and conundrums. No one knows much about its patterns of pathology yet, let alone its treatment spectrum. It's where big names are going to be made in the next ten or twenty years—and the more we understand about afterlife, hopefully, the more we'll understand about life. It's a very competitive field, but I'm hoping to go into it full-time when I'm fully qualified."

"Much competition from zombie doctors, is there?" I enquired, mildly. Rivalry between living and afterliving doctors was a significant minor theme on *Resurrection Ward*.

"Hardly any, as yet," he admitted. "The requalification

requirements are too tight. So far as I know, there aren't any afterliving doctors in England outside of London."

"Discrimination by any other name would smell as rank...." I murmured.

"It's a bit soon to be getting militant, Mr. Rosewell," he said, sternly, "but if marching on parliament's your thing, you'll probably feel right at home with the lunatic fringe at the Mount Pleasant Center. At any rate, we'd better see what we can do about getting you back on your feet a.s.a.p." And with that, he was off.

Nurse Pearl didn't get the promised laptop to me until just before lights out on day two, with strict instructions not to disturb the other patients with the glow of the screen or any sound-effects. By then, I was too tired to throw myself wholeheartedly into assiduous research. I didn't want to comb the web for information on the side-effects of zombification and the availability of local support services. I wanted to see Helena. Mum too, and Kirsten, and even Dad—but mostly Helena.

After lights out, I couldn't sleep, even though I'd meekly taken my prescribed sedative like a good boy.

It seemed a trifle unfair, somehow, that zombies needed sleep. Surely, I thought, that ought to have been an affliction of life, a larval matter...like weeping. I couldn't help wondering, though, whether my zombie dreams would be the same as the dreams of the living me, and whether the afterliving forgot their dreams just as easily as the living.

Everything was up for reappraisal; even phenomena that seemed the same, at first, might turn out in the fullness of time to be subtly different. I tried to convince myself that it was a really exciting prospect, but I was too tired.

Eventually, though, I did go to sleep—and if I dreamed, I forgot what I had dreamed as soon as I was awake.

I passed the following morning's psych evaluation with flying colors. It wasn't that much different from the others I'd undergone recently, by virtue of being certified as a civil service employee fit for face-to-face contact with members of the public. The trick is not to pretend to be absolutely normal, but to show tolerant awareness of one's own eccentricities, and to suppress one's natural inclination to make jokes. Like everyone else, I knew all about the trick questions designed to surprise latent schizophrenia or lurking Asperger's, and ducked them with ease.

I didn't feel guilty about cheating; arguably, there's no better proof of sanity than the ability to fake it. What is sanity, after all, but competent performance in the drama of life? Or after-life.

Once they'd had the ludicrously-delayed go-ahead, Mum and Dad came in together; inevitably, Mum started off doing most of the talking. She was every bit as wary as Dad, though—entirely understandably, given that I no longer looked like my old self, and that they too must have been poring over assorted websites for hours on end, reading horror stories about personality changes in the afterliving, and the awful prescience of *Frankenstein*.

"It's okay," I assured them, when the fussing had died away to an acceptable level—which didn't take long. "I died young, but not so young that my brain hadn't fully developed. I was complete, as a person, but still relatively fresh. There's no reason why the stem cells should have reconfigured my neural pathways to any significant extent—unlike my face, apparently. Who would have thought that faces were so malleable? Just think of it as fancy plastic surgery. How's Kirsty taking it."

"Quite well, all things considered," Mum assured me. "She's at work just now, but she'll pop in on her way home."

"And Helena?"

"I don't know. We haven't really seen much of Helena—our paths don't cross outside the hospital corridors. Your Gran and Uncle Bill sent their good wishes."

"Thank them for me," I said, absent-mindedly. "I expect I'll be out before the weekend—the hospital will want the bed. I'll have to come back to you initially, if that's okay, but I'll try not to out-stay my welcome. I'll get in touch with my landlord as soon as I can—I can't do it from here without a phone or email. I know my lease has been voided, technically, but that doesn't mean that he can't re-let the flat to me, and it would save him the hassle of finding a new tenant."

"We had to collect all your stuff," Dad put in. "I don't know if the flat's been re-let yet, but it's certainly been cleared out."

"It doesn't matter," Mum assured me. "You can stay with us as long as you want. I'm not having you going to any hostel. There's no rush about finding another place of your own." *If you can*, she was careful not to add.

"I suppose they sent you all my stuff from the office as well," I said.

"There wasn't much," Dad said, as if that might somehow be of comfort to me.

"No," I said. "Well, I'll be reapplying for my job as well. I've got the experience. In an open and fair competition, I'd be bound to get it."

"There's no rush," Mum repeated. "You'll need a rest first. I'll take a few days off myself, until you're settled. I've only got four days owing, mind, and I can't afford to lose pay. There's a program, though—the social worker explained it all to us. You'll be able to go to the local Afterlife Center every day—it's the old Salvation Army Hall, so it's only a short walk even if your Dad or I can't drive you. You'll get physio and counselling, and you'll be able to meet…." She trailed off, but then added: "The nurse seems nice." There was no ambiguity as to which nurse she meant.

"A veritable Pearl," I said. Nobody cracked a smile. "I passed the psych evaluation," I pointed out. "I'm certified *compos mentis*. Once I'm out, I'm out. Nobody can stop me trying to get my job back—and the flat."

"You can't get another flat until you get a job, son," Dad told me, sadly. "Even if we stumped up the deposit for you, you couldn't get a flat until you have a bank account, and you can't get a bank account until you have an income to feed it. The dole won't stretch, and the bank won't give you an account on the strength of a dole slip. I'm not sure you'll even be able to get a new phone, unless you get a pay-as-you-go model."

"All that may be true," I admitted, "but let's look on the bright side—my student loans have been cancelled along with my credit rating. How many people of my age can say that they're debt free, eh?"

"That's right," Mum hastened to agree. "You're better off than a lot of...." Again she left it at that.

I *was* better off than a lot of the recently reborn. Not many of the older afterliving had parents young enough to take them in and lend them support—and some of those who did were refused, even if they hadn't tacitly insulted their families by topping themselves. If Mum and Dad hadn't been willing to take me in, I would have ended up at the former Bail Hostel on South Street, which was now an Afterlife Hostel, conveniently located only a couple of hundred yards from the old Salvation Army Hall, now the local Afterlife Center—which was itself, presumably not entirely by virtue of coincidence, only half a mile from the Royal Berks Burking Unit. All very cosy.

"Anyway," Mum added, "you don't have to worry. You can stay as long as you like."

I knew, and she knew that I knew, that she wouldn't have said that if I'd still been alive, having just recovered from a conventional operation, because we'd all have taken it for granted, so it wouldn't have needed saying—but it didn't seem to matter. The fact was that it did need saying

"I feel fine," I assured her. "According to the internet, that's normal. Zombie convalescence is only protracted if there's been substantial neural reconfiguration. In my case, there hasn't. Clean death, clean afterlife, as they'll probably say once I've had time to establish it as a proverb." Nobody laughed, so I pressed on: "I passed all the tests. I'm okay—and I'm still the same person I always was. Top goalscorer, wicked wit." *Head over heels in love*, I didn't add—but not because it wasn't true.

"Of course you are, love," Mum said, with as much sincerity as she could muster.

Kirsten wasn't quite as vapid, when she eventually turned up. Sisters don't labor under the relentless pressure of parental responsibility. They can even be spiteful if they want to be. Mercifully, my darling Kirsty didn't. She wasn't a teenager any more, and even when she had been, she'd been a full paid-up member of Greenpeace.

"We've already had threats, you know," she said, when we'd managed to persuade Mum and Dad to go home.

"What threats?" I said. "Who from."

"They're not that specific," she said, "and they're not signed. The policewoman we called said that the black spot is from the ED—adapted from *Treasure Island*, apparently. It's a death-threat, but she said not to take it too seriously. England's Defenders apparently haven't got the manpower or the time to follow through on everyday threats of that sort. They have to be selective in planning their publicity stunts."

Kirsty was right, even if it was a trifle undiplomatic to say so. I'd been killed by a publicity stunt. I hadn't even been an innocent bystander at a purposive murder. I was collateral damage to a headline, and not much of one at that. Making a bang in the Oracle wasn't exactly blowing the dome off St. Paul's Cathedral, or flying a jumbo jet into Canary Wharf. It was a run-of-the mill firework in a run-of-the-mill shopping mall, which had killed seven run-of-the-mill passers-by. England's so-called Defenders didn't even have the manpower or the guts to keep up with the jihadists on a strict tit-for-tat basis.

"The bastards should have sent you flowers and an apology, never mind a black spot," I observed, with a sigh. "After all, they weren't targeting *us*, were they? If you and me and Mum and Dad aren't numbered among the True Britons they're supposed to be defending, who is? Our name's Rosewell, for God's sake."

"I'm in Greenpeace," she pointed out. "The ED don't like Greenpeace." *And you're a zombie*, she didn't add, though not because it wasn't true.

"Even so," I said, "given that they've already killed me, it seems a trifle churlish of them to threaten my afterlife. Who were the other threats from, do you think?"

"The rest are probably from religious nuts, but the policewoman who collected them says that people of that sort are far more likely to confine themselves to writing anonymous letters, saying ostentatious prayers and ranting in the street than to attempt physical violence—even the rabid jihadists are more urgently concerned with fighting manifest infidels than supposed demons."

"You'd think *they* might lay off too," I remarked, "given that it was their sworn enemies who killed me. If I'd been a Muslim, I'd have been a martyr, wouldn't I?"

"Not once you were reborn. When it comes to the crunch, some westernized Muslims do sign the consent form, but a lot refuse. You're right about that being a reason why the ED shouldn't be so down on zombies—I mean *the afterliving*. It's not just you—ninety per cent of the afterliving in Reading must have started off as so-called True Britons."

"It's okay," I said. "You can call me a zombie. Sisterly privilege. And don't worry about the threats—even if an ED hitman does get through to me, I'll be back again in no time."

"Second resurrections rarely work," she told me. "I looked it up."

So had I. "But I died young," I told her. "Resilience to spare. There's some guy in New Zealand who's already been resurrected three times—he was about the same age as me when he shuffled off his original mortal coil."

"I'd rather you didn't go for any world records," she said.

"I'm glad you care," I told her, sincerely.

She burst into tears, perhaps because she was mortally afraid that there might come a time when she couldn't.

"Have you seen Helena?" I asked her, when she'd wiped her eyes. "I was expecting her to come, as soon as she could."

"Not recently," she said.

"Maybe the hospital hasn't notified her that I'm conscious, because she's not a relative. Could you give her a ring, just to make sure that she knows?"

"Okay," she said, unenthusiastically. She didn't reach for her phone.

I had to let her off the hook—she was my sister. "She *has* been to see me," I told her. "Nurse Pearl said so—but you can leave it until later to phone her, if you want."

"I will," she promised—and hesitated before adding: "It might not be a good idea to hope for too much in that direction, Nicky."

"Hope doesn't come into it," I told her. "Everybody knows that true love lasts forever."

"Till death us do part," she quoted, quietly, as if slyly laying a trump on my ace in a game of Knockout Whist.

"This is the twenty-first century," I reminded her. "Death no longer parts." It was a weak reply, though. Death voided marriages as well as other kinds of contracts, even in the eyes of the church, let alone engagements and not-quite-engagements. According to the web, the number of marriages severed by death that had been voluntarily remade after rebirth was tiny—which didn't bode well for engagements, not-quite-engagements and simply being madly in love, even though there were no actual statistics available.

"I really need to talk to her," I added. "That's all."

"Sure," said Kirsten, in a way that suggested that she was anything but sure, about Helena or anything else.

"I still feel the same about her as I did before," I persisted, "Just as I feel the same way about you." I didn't suppose for a moment that my darling little sister was in doubt about that, but I thought it was worth emphasizing.

"Helena might not be able to feel the same way about you," she countered, reluctantly, as if she felt that she'd been forced into saying it for me because I couldn't bear to say it for myself.

"Are *you*?" I asked. It felt as though it slipped out, but I couldn't hep wondering whether that was what I'd being dying to ask all along, without being able to admit it to myself. "Is Dad? Is Mum?"

"That's not fair, Nicky," she replied, with deadly accuracy.

"Should I take that as a no, then?" I demanded, compounding the unfairness.

She started crying again, and this time didn't try to wipe her eyes. "I'm on your side," she told me, resentfully. "I'll *always* be on your side. We all will."

I didn't doubt it for a moment. Even so, it didn't answer the question, did it?

CHAPTER FOUR

It's a commonplace of sociology that the self is a social product. It's all very well for Rabbie Burns to remark that, if we could only see ourselves as others see us, it would free us from many a blunder and foolish notion; the sad fact is that the ability we have to insulate ourselves from the gaze of others by means of the armor of delusion is strictly limited. By and large, we have little alternative but to see ourselves as others see us, and little opportunity to take any grievances that may arise to any Ombudsman capable of winning us a reappraisal.

Or, to put it simply—even though it really isn't as simple as that—if people see you as a zombie, you really don't have much alternative to being what they believe a zombie to be.

You can resist, of course. You can make your stand—be a valiant Knight of the Living Dead, as the hoariest pun in today's world puts it—but that makes you into Don Quixote, not Sir Lancelot, in the eyes of others. As soon as you start tilting, you realize that those bloody windmills really are giants, and that your chances of bringing any of them down are pretty damn slim.

You shouldn't get bitter about it, though. Every living person who condescends to speak to you will tell you that. You should, in fact, be grateful for a second lease of life. Even now, most of the living don't get one. Even now, most of the dead stay dead. SSCs can only do so much. The best way to guarantee yourself an afterlife, if that's your ambition, is to kill yourself carefully. Letting nature do the job for you is too risky.

Ironic, eh?

It's foolish to blame others for seeing you as a different person, though, once you've passed on, because you really are a different person. They're right, and if you don't think so, you're wrong. Even if it were just the albinism, that would be enough… but you know as well as they do that it's so much more. Nobody knows exactly why, but that's the way it is.

Given that zombies are genotypically identical to their previous selves, there's no obvious reason why they should be unable to produce melanin in their skin cells, or tears in their eyes, or why they should mostly be slightly less able to metabolize lipids and slightly better able to metabolize proteins, or why they should mostly be seemingly immune to the common cold and many kinds of cancer but not to gonorrhoea or syphilis, or why they should mostly be subject to any manner of other subtle modifications, some of which have doubtless yet to be discovered. Opinions, as the most basic internet search reveals, are very varied and deeply divided.

At first, I was attracted to the sober explanations, which focused on gene-switching. Even "identical" twins, it seems, begin to accumulate differences as soon as the original ovum divides, because embryological development has its idiosyncrasies. Genes switched on in particular tissues of one twin are sometimes switched off in some or all of the other twin's relevant tissues. Obviously, the key differences between the living and the afterliving are much more consistent than that, so they must be caused by some aspect of the rejuvenative process by which superstimulant stem cells are produced, but the way those differences take effect has to be determined by particular genes being switched on or off in particular tissues. Even the totipotent stem cells regenerated for the treatment of the living don't necessarily reproduce the same patterns of function as the cells of the mature body from which their ancestors are taken, and superstimulant stem cells are more potent still, as they obviously have to be.

In theory, two egg-cells with exactly the same stock of genes could produce vastly different phenotypes, depending upon the order in which genes are activated as the embryo develops; perhaps the real wonder is that SSCs produce something so nearly similar to the living individual. The similarities are, in fact, greater than they appear; it isn't that zombies don't produce any melanin at all, but rather that they produce it in a more limited spectrum of tissues, while producing an alternative protein in superficial tissues, which happens to be colorless. All things considered, therefore, the variant switching theory requires very little in the way of hypothetical elaboration; in the judgment of Occam's razor, it wins hands down against its rivals, most of which tend to the bizarre.

In the beginning, I was inclined to shy away from the bizarre. Sometimes, habits die harder than life itself.

* * * * * * *

There were yet more tests, of course, and the doctors had to make sure that I could cope with solid food again, but it quickly became obvious that the NHS needed my bed more than I did, so they only kept me in for observation for one more night. Mum brought the car to pick me up at eleven o'clock the next morning, when all the formalities had been sorted.

I made a point to saying goodbye to Nurse Pearl, who simply sighed and said: "You'll be seeing a lot more of me, I fear, Nicky. Andy too—whenever we're not here or asleep, we're practically always at the Center."

I hadn't told her that she could call me "Nicky," but she'd obviously heard my parents using that particular diminutive. Dr. Hazelhurst's first name was Andrew; I didn't know whether he'd given her permission to cal him that, or whether she'd just heard other doctors doing it. "I might not be there that often myself," I said. "After all, I've got a home to go to."

"Trust me, Nicky," she said, "you will be seeing more of me. It doesn't matter a damn whether either of us likes the idea, or not."

"It's fine by me," I hastened to assure her. She didn't reciprocate, and she didn't help me to smear on and rub in my factor-32, even though she was a nurse, and it was probably part of her job-description.

After I'd done the smearing and rubbing for myself, I walked over to the guy with the index fingers. "It was very kind of you to send me so many plus signs," I told him. "I really appreciated the kind thought, and the innovative enterprise—the old thumbs-up is *so* passé."

I don't think he understood what *passé* meant, but that wasn't why he didn't laugh at the joke.

Mum had brought me a set of clothes selected from the stuff that Dad had cleared out of my flat—including a woolly jumper, even though it was twenty-seven degrees outside. Mercifully, she'd also brought a brand new broad-brimmed hat, cotton gloves and sunglasses. The hospital had presumably given her a list.

I couldn't sit still in the car; I had a bad case of restless leg syndrome. While I was alive, I'd always thought of restless leg syndrome as one of those ingenious notions invented by pharmaceutical companies because it's so much easier to invent effective cures for imaginary diseases than real ones, but it's real. Even zombies can get it.

"I'll need to use your phone and email account, temporarily," I said to Mum. "I need to contact the OO, to let them know I'll be reapplying, and I ought to notify the lads in the footy team that I'll be available when training for the new season starts, in case they're worried…and I need to let Helena know where I am. It's okay if she comes to the house when she finishes work, isn't it?"

"If she wants to," Mum said, evidently doubting it. Like Kirsten, she seemed to know more than I did about the reasons why Helen hadn't returned to the hospital to visit me once I'd woken up—and like Kirsten, she wasn't about to tell me what she knew, or how.

"It's probably better than me going round to her place," I

said, deliberately misunderstanding Mum's cautionary reservation. "Her flat-mate will probably be there, and she didn't like me much when I was alive. I really need to talk to her—Helena, that is, not her flat-mate."

"Don't expect too much too soon," Mum said, diplomatically.

I really did think that she was being overly cautious, especially when I eventually got through to Helena on the borrowed phone, and she agreed to come round to the house to see me as soon as she finished work. I thought, judging by the sound of her beloved voice, that everything was going to be all right.

On the other hand, when I phoned the captain of my Sunday Morning League team to tell him that his star striker was well on the way to recovery and would available for pre-season training in spite of no longer being alive, and he told me how glad he was, and how he'd be sure to send me an email, I didn't believe a word he said—any more than I believed the exceedingly polite and well-spoken guy in the call-center in Mumbai when he assured me that the Ombudsman's Office would welcome my application to fill the vacancy presumably left by my death, and would give it their most sympathetic consideration.

Helena was a primary school teacher, so it wasn't very late when she arrived at my parents' house—she was well in advance of Dad and Kirsten getting back from work, on the doorstep on the dot of four. I only made a half-hearted attempt to kiss her as she came in, and tried not to read too much into the fact that she avoided the clinch.

"I'm sorry I couldn't contact you from the hospital," I said, while Mum went to make a pot of tea. "They gave me a laptop so I could search the web, but all my communication credit's been cancelled. I could have borrowed Kirsty's phone last night, but I wanted to see you face to face. Anyway, I figured that you might need some notice, if the hospital hadn't notified you that I was conscious, on account of your not being family, technically speaking. Did Kirsty ring you?"

"Yes, she did," Helena confirmed.

"Good. I thought it would be best to meet here. Have you

missed me?"

"Of course," she said.

"I wasn't gone that long, though," I said. I'd worked out that this was only the twenty-third day since the bomb-blast. "We're still okay, aren't we?"

Her silence spoke volumes. I didn't want to press the point immediately.

"There's no need to worry," I told her. "I'm still the same person I was before. No substantial brain-damage, you see. A glass dagger in the heart—quick and clean. Externally singed, but not internally pulverized. I was just far enough away, thank God—I must have been taking a short cut back to the office after stopping in at the library on my lunch break. I wasn't shopping…even if I had been, my masculine instincts would have made me give TK Maxx a wide berth."

She smiled, but it was forced. "I did come to see you," she told me, adding—entirely gratuitously, in my opinion—"to say goodbye."

"I was unconscious," I reminded her.

"You were dead," she countered.

"And now I'm not."

"No," she admitted, "you're not…but it's not the same, Nicky."

She stopped, and again her silence spoke volumes. I wasn't going to let her off the hook, though. I waited for what I was due.

"I thought I owed it to you to come and tell you in person," she said, finally, "because it would have been cowardly not to, but I can't. I just can't."

There was no point in asking her to specify what it was that she couldn't. There were tears in the corners of her eyes, but none in mine. There was no point, either, in repeating that I was still the same person that I was before, whether it was true or not. The point was that I didn't appear to be.

"I still love you," I told her, "with all my heart."

"I know," she said, weakly—although she couldn't know,

really.

"I always will," I told her.

She wasn't even going to pretend to know, or believe that, or even to take it seriously.

"I can't, Nicky," she said, again. "I thought I could, for a day or two. I honestly tried. But I can't. You died. And you came back—but coming back isn't the same as not going. I can't."

"Maybe if we got to know one another again…start afresh…." I said. Maybe that was when I first began to develop a taste for the bizarre. It sounded ridiculous, even to me.

"No, Nicky," she said. "It's over. I'm sorry, but that's the way it is. I have to go now."

"You haven't drunk your tea."

"I know."

It should have ended there, but it didn't. There's no point in reproducing the rest, though. It wouldn't show me in a good light, and as it's my story, I reserve the right not to do that, so long as I don't actually falsify anything. Sometimes, the abbreviated truth is better than the whole truth and nothing but the truth. And even if it's not…well, as I say, it's my story, and I'll tell it the way I want to.

The way I want to tell it is that I was still in love with Helena, and convinced I always would be, but that it really wasn't her fault that she couldn't reciprocate any longer. After all, it wasn't as if we were engaged to be married, or even almost-engaged. No promises had been made, no sworn undertakings given. We'd simply been in love, and now one of us wasn't, any longer.

And for once, in spite of everything I could do to resist the fact, it really was as simple as that.

When Helena had finally gone home, Mum came in, and tried to put her arm around me. She couldn't—perhaps because I was grown up now, no longer a child.

"That's the way it is," I told her.

For once, she had nothing to say.

"It doesn't need to be," I told her. "If we could just…pull ourselves together. I'm only a couple of shades paler than I was before, for God's sake! I don't even have to wear the hat and sunglasses indoors. It's next to nothing. I'm not Frankenstein's fucking monster."

"Of course not," she said, not bothering to complain about my intemperate language. "You're the same person you were before. She doesn't deserve you. You'll find someone else. That nurse liked you, I think."

There was no need whatsoever to ask which nurse, and no earthly point in pointing out that Pearl had shown no evidence of any such liking.

"I think she's in love with Dr. Hazelhurst," I said.

"What makes you think that?" Mum asked, warily.

"All nurses fall in love with doctors," I said. "If soap operas teach us nothing else, they teach us that. And she calls him Andy. He's not in love with her, of course. He'll break her heart. Doctors always break nurses' hearts. If soap operas teach us nothing else, they teach us that. The fact that she's a zombie and he's not is irrelevant, in this instance."

"Well if that's the case," Mum said, probably not in the least deceived as to what we were really talking about, "he doesn't deserve her, and she'll find someone else."

"A Pearl before swine," I muttered, pointlessly. I didn't smile. Nor did Mum.

Kirsten arrived home then, but I couldn't bear to talk to her. I never even saw Dad that evening. I needed to be alone with my burning, brooding, tragically unrequited love.

It was still burning and brooding the next morning, but I no longer needed to be alone, and certainly not with Mum, even though she was still off work.

"I'm going to the Center at the old Sally Ann," I told her, when breakfast as out of the way. "Got to introduce myself, find out what's what."

"I'll drive you," she said.

"Don't be silly—it's only a few hundred yards. I've got to make a start on facing up to the world, facing up to reality. I need to show my face—let the neighbors get used to it. I need to walk."

"You only got out of hospital yesterday," she protested. "You *died*, Nicky. I don't care how well you feel—you *died*."

I knew that, but I could understand why she felt obliged to emphasize the point.

"I know, Mum," I said, quietly. "But I'm up and about again now. I have to make new beginning. I need to start making some new friends...because it wouldn't be fait to put too much pressure on the old ones, would it?"

"I'm your mother," she said, although I hadn't actually accused her of anything. "I still love you, as much as I ever did. I always will."

"I know, Mum," I told her, "but I still need to go to the Center, and I'd really like to walk. I'm a Knight of the Living Dead now: I have to undergo my trials by ordeal, or I'll never get to touch the Holy Grail, let alone drink lemonade out of it."

She didn't smile—but she didn't shed a tear either.

"Be careful," she said.

"I will," I promised—and I was.

Actually, there wasn't any real need to be careful. I didn't see a single rottweiler taking his ED member out for a walk, and most of the non-white faces I passed in the street, including the "white" ones, simply looked the other way, with a kind of feigned negligence that seemed oddly polite, in its fashion. There were exceptions, though—mostly people I met before I got to the end of the street, who had known me when I lived at home, before I went away to university. They knew who I was, in spite of my changed appearance, and some of them made a point of saying hello, or at least nodding. I was grateful for that.

Once I'd turned the corner, though, it was different. I'd been sent to Coventry. I almost regretted the fact that no one even made a sign of the cross with his index-fingers, let alone hurled holy water at me and shouted in Latin, or do whatever Muslims do when they're attempting to repel evil djinn.

It wasn't all bad, though. I started to make new friends even before I reached the double-doors of the old Salvation Army

Hall, catching up and falling into step with two members of the afterliving—one a middle-aged female and one an old man—who were headed in the same direction, coming from the direction of the old Bail Hostel in South Street. It was obvious, even from behind, what they were, because of the broad-brimmed hats.

"Hi," I said. "I'm Nick Rosewell."

They paused, and peered at me through their dark glasses.

"But your friends call you Nicky," the woman said. "Pearl told us to expect you. I'm Marjorie, and this is Martin—but *his* friends call him Methuselah."

I could see why. Marjorie looked as if she'd died in her late forties, but Martin-alias-Methuselah must have been at least seventy when he'd passed over. *Poor old sod,* I thought. *Condemned to look seventy-five forever. It's like that old saw about your features getting stuck if the wind happens to change while you're pulling a face.*

"*Everybody* calls me Methuselah," the old man added. "I don't mind in the least—it gives me something to aim for."

"Aim for?" I queried, although I really shouldn't have been caught on the hop.

"*And Methuselah lived an hundred and eighty and seven years,*" he quoted, sententiously, "*and begat Lamech*...except that I'm not so sure about begetting Lamech. I'll settle for the years."

"Right," I said. "I can see that I'm going to feel at home at the Center. Are you members of what Dr. Hazelhurst referred to as the *lunatic fringe?*"

"Not me," said Methuselah. "Marjorie is—although it's slightly cheeky of you to ask."

"I can see that you're going to be a veritable treasure," Marjorie assured me. "We don't have many young people, and it's no bad thing to be cheekier than Jim. He's a nice chap, but I must admit that I find his constant pessimism annoying. We'll all *love* you." She didn't specify exactly who she meant by *all*.

"That's nice," I said, "but I've already got a girl-friend." I just slipped out. It wasn't *exactly* a lie. After all, I was still in love.

"Well then, I'll have my work cut out, won't I?" Marjorie said. "I've never minded a bit of competition, though. And I always get my man." She smiled—and the smile, although it was a trifle hollow, made her look rather attractive. She might have been slightly intimidating in life, but the paleness of afterlife had softened her strong features a little, and she had a good figure, robust but shapely.

"She's teasing," Methuselah supplied, helpfully. "She means the bit about not being intimidated by competition, though—that's why Andy makes patronizing remarks about the lunatic fringe. She was famous you know, in life, and she's gradually fighting her way back to the top."

Marjorie seemed a trifle ambivalent about that revelation, but she took it in good part. "You won't have heard of me," she said. "Marjorie Claridge. I was…."

"A mouthpiece for Greenpeace," I put, swiftly. "My sister's a keen member. She'll be tickled pink to know that I've met you—I don't think she has any idea that you're in Reading."

"I post anonymously these days," Marjorie said, "and keep my address secret. Not that I like lying low…it's just that my old friends, grateful as they are for my continued support…well, it's complicated."

I nodded sympathetically. "I understand," I said, thinking, in my naivety, that I did.

We had reached the steps of the Hall already. The words SALVATION ARMY were still engraved in the sandstone lintel above the sturdy double door. There wasn't even a piece of paper pinned to the batten to inform passers-by or new members that it was now an Afterlife Center.

"Have you met Stan yet?" Methuselah asked, as climbed the four steps leading up to the doors.

"No," I said. "Pearl mentioned him, though. He runs the place, right?"

"He thinks he does" Marjorie murmured, as we opened one of the battens of the double door and slipped through. "And we humor him, poor lamb."

She was joking, of course. Stan came to meet me as soon as he realized that he had a newcomer to add to his flock. A lamb he was not, and not just because he must have been at least sixty when he died. He was an alpha ram from top to toe. He wasn't that much taller than me—no more than five-eleven, I estimated—but he was very solidly build and looked very tough indeed, in spite of his albinism. He had a shaven head and a nose that looked as if it had been broken more than once. He was wearing track-suit bottoms and a black T-shirt, which exposed numerous tattoos on both upper arms. *Dragons two, roses three,* I though, quoting it to myself like a football score.

Aloud, all I said was: "Pleased to meet you—I'm Nick Rosewell."

"And your friends call you Nicky," he said, putting the seal on my fate. "Pearl told us to expect you. I'm Stanley Blake—Stan to my friends. We'll be starting rockmobility in a quarter of an hour or so, but there's time for Methuselah to show you round first, if he doesn't mind."

"I don't mind," Methuselah said. "I don't have to do retraining programs, like the younger folk, so I have more free time," he added, by way of explanation. "Not that I still get my pension, of course—I'm on minimal dole, just like everyone else."

"There's not much to see, I'm afraid," Stan resumed, "except for the workstations…you can use them for your retraining courses, if you want…although I gather that you've got a home to go to."

"I'm staying with my parents for now," I confirmed, although I really wanted to ask him what "rockmobility" might be. "I've got a workstation there—it used to be in my flat but…well, you understand."

"Sure," said Stan. "Don't worry—you'll be at home here too. You look pretty fit, for a newreborn—sportsman?"

"Just Sunday Morning football in Palmer Park—soccer, that is. I hear you've got a rugby player."

"Jim Peel," Stan confirmed, looking round but obviously

not spotting the prop forward in question. "Did some weights myself, a long time ago, a little boxing—no good with my feet though…not for kicking, anyway."

"Much better at tripping the light fantastic, no doubt?" I quipped.

He grinned wryly. "You've been talking to Pearl," he said, seemingly jumping to an erroneous conclusion. "Don't take her sarcasm too seriously. She can be sharp, but her heart's in absolutely the right place."

"Never doubted it," I assured him, with perfect candor.

Stan excused himself then, handing me back to Methuselah. Marjorie Claridge had already slipped away, apparently having spotted a vacant workstation.

As Stan had said, there wasn't a lot to see. The Hall itself was moderately large—about thirty meters by twenty-five, but it was a trifle bare, apart from the mezzanine where the workstations had been installed. There was a small kitchenette, with a serving-hatch, but it didn't have much in it except for a sink, a couple of cupboards, a coffee-maker and a microwave oven. There was also a store-room, off the corridor that led to the back door, but we didn't go in to inspect it.

"Stan sleeps in there, although he isn't supposed to, according to the Council regs," Methuselah explained. "There's a second bunk, in case of emergencies, but the Hostel's only a couple of hundred yards away, so it doesn't get used much. Most of the gang live there, although Jim stays with his parents, like you, and those who have jobs mostly have their own places… not Pearl though; she lives in the accommodation-block at the Berks—what they used to call a "nurses' home" in my young days, although that's not politically correct now that junior doctors use it too. And this is Stan's blaster."

Stan's "blaster"—an old fashioned audio unit with twin speakers nearly as tall as me, was the only substantial item of furniture on the floor of the hall, except for a handful of tatty armchairs and two trestle-tables, each with half a dozen folding chairs presently laid flat on top of them.

"Rockmobility," Methuselah said, as if that explained everything. Obviously, he thought Pearl had told me as much about the Center as she'd apparently told the people in the Center about me. Lowering his voice, he added: "We'll spread the chairs out later, when Stan's done his thing—make the place more comfortable. Have to humor him, though, as Marjorie says."

"He thinks he runs the place," I observed, flippantly. "Poor lamb."

CHAPTER FIVE

I'd lied to my mother in the heat of the moment; I *was* Frankenstein's monster. I had been brought back from the dead. End of story.

I hadn't been stitched together from spare parts of other people's bodies, but I'd been stitched together from the debris of my own. I had died. My heart had stopped; brain activity had faded to undetectability. Consciousness—the soul, in the only meaningful sense of the word—had fled its mortal envelope, leaving nothing but a husk. Then I had been reanimated: brought back, if not to life, at least to a condition resembling life, and to a condition seemingly identical to consciousness. Frankenstein's monster to a T.

According to the pope himself, I no longer had a soul—the one I'd had was now "with God". Mind you, it wasn't that long ago since once of the jolly old soul's predecessors had ruled that human clones couldn't possibly have souls, thus condemning half of every pair of identical twins to soullessness. None of them had minded; why should I?

In any case, the real point is that even Frankenstein's monster had only become a monster because other people rejected him, refusing to consider him one of their own. Had he not been rejected, even by his creator—a poor excuse for a modern Prometheus *he* was—the Adam of the Resurrected might have been good and kind, mild and generous, loving and caring. Just like me.

I *was* Frankenstein's monster, but there was no need at all to be ashamed of the fact—and I wasn't.

Except, of course that it wasn't as simple as that.

There was, after all, a sense in which I *hadn't* been dead—not entirely, at any rate. When the heart has ceased to beat and the brain to thrill with electricity, and consciousness has fled, life still remains in individual cells within individual tissues—and every one of those cells carries the entire genetic complement of the human being of which it is, or was, a part. In principle, every one of those cells might, by means of clever biotech wizardry, be reduced to pre-blastular innocence, to become not merely a totipotent stem cell but a substitute ovum, merely requiring a tiny electrical impulse to spark its redevelopment.

Today's Burkers don't cut it as fine as that. They work on a more lavish scale, They take, not one, but a thousand still-living cells from a body whose *person*—soul, if you like—is dead, restore their innocence, enhance their potency, and then send them back into the not-quite-completely-dead body like a vast invading army. There they collaborate with other still-living cells, reanimating the only-just-dead and cannibalizing the irredeemably-dead, all in the interests of restoring general life and general consciousness to the whole body, restarting the heart-beat, reactivating the thrill of the neurons and, in consequence, resurrecting the person, and maybe renewing the soul.

In a sense, therefore, the dead are not being *brought back* to life at all; it's merely the life that still remained within them, helpless and fugitive, that has been rescued, redeemed and set free again. The processs isn't a death followed by an afterlife at all, but a mere temporary diminution of life, followed by its reignition: medicine, not magic; heroic measures, not miracle-working.

Nevertheless, it would be a brave and foolhardy zombie who could look a living man in the dark and sullen eyes and say: "I am no monster. I am no different from you." Because we *are* different—and if we are made to be monsters by rejection, then we will monsters too. It isn't our choice, but our destiny.

I guess the point I'm trying to make is that it's really up to *you*.

You might think, dear reader, that you're personally guiltless, that it wasn't *you*, as such, who made Frankenstein's monster into a monster: that it was really Mary Shelley, or the way of the world. Even if you recognized the *real* villains when you read the book or watched the movie, though, there's still a sense in which you share in the responsibility, because it's your world that it's the way of, and your preconceptions that Mary Shelley was taking for granted and interrogating. You can't get off the hook simply by protesting that your own hands are blood-free, because you've just washed them.

Perhaps you don't care—after all, you have a choice as to whether to care or not, and who am I to say that you should?

* * * * * * *

If I said that the Afterlife Center was jam-packed with friendly faces, I wouldn't be telling the whole truth, although most of them made a sterling effort. Arguably, I'd got the best first.

Methuselah really was keen to tell me anything I wanted to know, because that was the role he'd adopted along with his nickname: in life, he had only been a run-of-the-mill pensioner named Martin Creston; in afterlife, he was Methuselah, Zombie Rehab's archetypal Wise Old Man. I liked him.

Marjorie was effusively friendly, when she could actually tear herself away from her anonymous propagandizing—not so much, I assumed, because she fancied my youthful zombie body, although she put on a flirtatious pretence, but because she really was a committed believer in the necessity of community and mutual support. I liked her too.

Stan really did want everyone to feel at home, because it was his Center and his flock, and he wanted everything to run smoothly and go with a swing...which was, I suppose, the logic of rockmobility. I even liked rockmobility, once I'd found out what it was.

One of the things that the Afterlife Center's program was

supposed to provide, according to what Methuselah called "the Council regs," was "physiotherapy." Very few zombies came through the process of rebirth as smoothly as I had, mainly because the great majority were so much older, and had suffered much greater deterioration in life. In most cases, their tissues required much more radical rebuilding than mine had. A lot of them came out of their "pupation" with muscles that were, in effect, new: unpractised and untrained. I still felt like me, physically as well as mentally, but even zombies who remained convinced that their souls had made the transfer from life to afterlife relatively unscathed often felt that they had been reborn into new bodies that were in dire need of exercise.

"Exercise" was a more accurate term than "physiotherapy," for what we actually got, if not what we really needed. There were no ex-trained physiotherapists among the zombies of Reading, and the living physiotherapists attached to the local Hospital Trust were occupied more than full-time with the needs of the living. What we had instead was Stanley Blake.

No one, so far as I could ascertain, knew exactly what Stan had done in life—apart from "a few weights" and "a little boxing"—but the most popular hypotheses were that he had either been a drill sergeant in the army or a professional dancer. Personally, I thought both guesses were absurd. No self-respecting drill-sergeant or dancing pro would ever have invented a monstrosity like rockmobility, which consisted of doing complex sequences of physical exercises, admittedly involving a lot of jumping around that might have borne a faint resemblance to street-dancing, to the accompaniment of loud, driving music.

Stan was a Classic Rock fan, and not just any Classic Rock. He was a Heavy Metal man—an old headbanger. He wasn't old enough to remember the heyday of Heavy Metal—even Methuselah would have been closer to the cradle than his teens back then—but that only meant that he had a true scholar's sense of completism, that he felt capable not only of knowing everything about it but of a kind of definitive appreciation of its merits and uses. The fact that no one else agreed with him didn't bother him in the least; his affection was truly religious—although that was a distinctly ironic observation, when one considered the titles of some of his favorite tracks.

Marjorie Claridge had just been modest when she'd owned up to being a member of the Center's lunatic fringe. By the time I'd been in the Center for two hours, I knew that as long as Stan thought he was in charge, lunacy would be not be in short supply.

Stan scheduled two hours of rockmobility every morning except Sundays—which meant that everybody who was present, from Methuselah to Pearl, had to line up facing him, and copy his hectic but strangely rhythmic movements to the best of their ability, until they dropped from exhaustion, while the voices of testosterone-crazed young men echoed from the walls and screeched incomprehensibly in their ears.

It was bizarre, but I have to admit that I really did like it, if only because I could do it—better, at least, than almost everyone else. I could claim no moral credit for that—it was simply a matter of age and the fact that my muscles and nerves had survived the ED suicide-bomb almost unscathed—but it still made me feel good. By the end of the week, I was a convert to the cause, even though I didn't really like the music that much. I could see the point.

"The thing is," Stan explained, once he had cottoned on to the fact that I was ready to sympathize with him, "that there are certain respects in which we're not like the living, and we not only have to accept that but make the most of it. The living all start off as babes in arms, and then they age, at a more-or-less steady rate. If they look after themselves, they can stay fit, even into their sixties and their seventies—hell, I've known eighty-year-olds who could still cut it down the gym…God, I wish we had a gym of our own, but….well, maybe someday, if Marjorie can get the banners flying….

"The point is, though, that we're in a different situation entirely. We don't start off equal. The law might be changed soon to lower the age of eligibility from eighteen to sixteen, but nobody's in any hurry to start turning out afterlifer babies who'll be permanently stuck in infancy, so we start afterlife from various points in a spectrum that extends from earliest adulthood all the way through to Methuselah's age, and there's a sense in which we're stuck with that. God knows why—it would be a lot pleasanter, I guess, if we got rejuvenated as well as resurrected, so that we all ended up your age, but we don't, and that's that….

"Anyway, there's a world of difference between a living person of sixty-one and an afterlifer whose death-date was sixty-one, like me. I'm just as ugly now as I was before, but I not *aging* any longer…or, if I am, not as fast. I'm not prepared to take it for granted that I can stay this way forever, if I'm careful enough and lucky enough, but I'm damned if I can see any reason why I shouldn't make the absolute best of myself for as long as superhumanly possible. The living can throw in the towel if they want to, and just let *getting older* take its course, but we needn't, and we shouldn't, no matter where or when we start from. We *can* get fit, no matter what age of death we started from, and we can *stay* fit…even if we're as old as Methuselah, let alone sixty-one. You see what I'm getting at, don't you, Son? We don't even know what we might be capable of yet, physically speaking, so we *have* to do our damnedest to push ourselves. We have to exercise—we have to dance.

"You get my point, don't you, Nicky. You understand why I'm doing this for the group?"

"Yes I do," I told him.

"And you see the logic of the hard-driving beat? You see why we need to stomp as hard as we can, and get the rhythm pounding in our chests, instead of prancing around to *pretty* music?"

"I'm not entirely sure that the words of *Highway to Hell* convey the right message," I opined, mildly, "but I see what you mean."

"It's a Classic," he said, with an injured frown. "The words are ironic."

"And I appreciate the irony," I assured him.

Once I was free again, Dr. Hazelhurst sidled up to me and whispered: "Teacher's pet." He had turned up five minutes after rockmobility was due to finish, although nobody had actually lasted the full two hours except Stan himself, and even Stan wasn't crazy enough to carry on stomping on his own. The chairs had already been spread out, and the beneficiaries of Stan's crude physiotherapy were slumped in them, making a gradual recovery.

"I'm just the new guy," I said. "It's kind of him to take the trouble to explain. Do you come here often?"

"Oh yes," he said. "Three or four times a week, at least. Research."

"Research?" I queried.

"Unfunded research," he amplified, proudly. "On my own time."

"Very impressive," I commented, as that seemed to be what he was fishing for.

"Oh, it's not because I'm possessed by a spirit of generosity," he hastened to add, obviously feeling that false modesty was likely to go over better than false arrogance. "I'm doing it because it's a good career move. The lack of official funding lessens the competition, and the field's wide open, as I told you back at the Berks. I'm limited, of course, in the kinds of research I can do—access to equipment and all that—but simply having a sample available, at this stage of the game, is invaluable. It's too small as yet to be really useful—Reading's quite a small town, geographically speaking—but as it grows…anyway, I'm hoping to add you to my roster of volunteers. You'd be invaluable."

"All guinea-pigs are equal," I told him. "I can't possibly be any more invaluable than anyone else, so flattery will get you nowhere. What's in it for me, if you're the one who gets to be famous if and when you find something interesting?"

"Come on, Nicky—you're a smart fellow, even if you do only

have a degree in English Lit. You know perfectly well that every afterliving individual has an interest in the speed of discovery being cranked up to the max. The more we know about afterlife, the better-placed the afterliving will be to make all the crucial decisions in afterlife…and the cleverer the Resurrection Men will become in saving people from permanent death, before *and* after." He meant that not only would Burkers be able to zombify more dead people, but that they'd become better able to preserve the zombified from whatever it was zombies did instead of dying, if they were careless enough to fall victim to nasty accidents.

"I'm flattered that you bothered to look up my educational qualifications," I told him. "I might only have a degree in English Lit, but I'm not stupid enough to volunteer without knowing what I'm volunteering for. Any experimental sample you want to include me in, you'll have to explain exactly what it is you're doing and why—and to hell with double blinds and the placebo effect."

"No problem Nicky," he assured me, blithely. "I'll take that as a yes, then. In principle."

"As Stan says," I told him, "we don't know what we're capable of yet, so we have to do our damnedest to find out, and hope that we're only on a Highway to Hell in an ironic sense—so yes, I'll help, provided that I know what I'm helping with."

"Great," he said. "Pearl said I could count on you—she's a good judge."

"You're just saying that because she's in love with you." It just slipped out—but it didn't seem out of place in the bantering context.

He frowned: "Who told you that?" he asked, sharply.

"Nobody," I said. "I guessed. I watch *Resurrection Ward*."

"Well, don't," he said, meaning don't guess rather than don't watch *Resurrection Ward*. "And don't say anything like that to Pearl, even in jest. She won't think it's funny."

"Okay," I agreed, meekly.

"She'll probably be in later, when her shift finishes."

"I'm sure she'll be heartbroken to have missed rockmobility," I said, trying to restore the balance of banter.

He condescended to smile. "It may be bizarre," he said, "but it does work. To be honest, Blake's doing a great job—if my tracking measurements show little else, as yet, they confirm that. Some of the people here really are in need of rehab, and he's getting the job done, without any equipment whatsoever. He's a good man."

"Never doubted it," I said.

Nurse Pearl did turn up later, in the early evening. By then, I'd discovered that her surname was Barleigh, suggesting that her parents had either been possessed of a wry sense of humor or none at all—probably the latter, given that they seemed to have taken such offense at her suicide that they'd virtually disowned her. Like Stan, she was regarded as more like a member of staff than an inmate—as the Center's medical practitioner and Andy Hazelhurst's research assistant—although she had no official status that would have allowed her to get paid for any such responsibility. She obviously took the same view of the necessities of our new society as Stan.

I tried to strike up a conversation with her, but she was too busy. She told me that she was glad to see me, and hoped that I was settling in, but didn't seem to have anything else to say. I concluded that, whether she was in love with Dr. Hazelhurst or not, she certainly wasn't going to start giving me the eye any time soon. Not that it mattered.

By the time I went back home on that first day I felt that Marjorie and Methuselah had been right. I did seem to fit in at the Center, even though there was no one there that would have had anything obvious in common with me when we were alive, and in spite of the fact that not everyone was as open-hearted as Methuselah, Marjorie and Stan. They all had problems of their own to preoccupy them; I understood that.

As I'd anticipated, Kirsten was both surprised and pleased when I told her that I'd met Marjorie Claridge.

"I thought she was dead and gone!" she said. "I didn't even

know she'd been resurrected, let alone that she was in Reading. She didn't live here before. Maybe she's in hiding."

"She doesn't seem to be," I said. "She'd surely be using a different name if she were. She did say that she posts anonymously these days, mind. Why would she be in hiding?"

"You do know that she was murdered?"

I hadn't. "Something else we have in common, then," I remarked.

"Something else?" Kirsten queried, sceptically. "You were never a Greenpeace member."

I'd only mean that we were both afterliving, and was mildly surprised that Kirsten hadn't realized that, but I felt obliged to follow up. "Oh, we're bosom buddies now," I said. "She fancies me—but she would, wouldn't she, given that I'm the best looking bloke there. Jim Peel's no competition, even though he's pretty much the same age. He was a rugby player."

"Marjorie Claridge fancies *you*?"

"Absolutely. Inevitable, as I say. I was fanciable before, although you probably didn't notice, being my little sister—but now, I'm practically a rock star, and not just for lack of opposition. You should see me doing physical jerks to *Highway to Hell*. Enough to make any red-blooded zombie woman wet her knickers…and believe you me, there are some frustrated zombie ladies up at the old Salvation Army Hall. Afterlife is a better pepper-upper than HRT."

She hesitated, actually uncertain as to whether to believe me or not.

"I'm joking," I assured her, swiftly. "It's me, Kirsty—wicked wit, remember."

She practically sighed with relief, although what she actually said was; "I knew that. I'm not an idiot."

It wasn't until later, when I was in bed reviewing my day before trying to go to sleep, that it occurred to me to remember that there's many a true word spoken in jest. No matter how fanciable I'd been, comparatively speaking, when I was alive, I really was in a situation now where I had very little opposition, and it really was the case that my apparent youth put me in a special position in the afterlife community. I'd discussed the minority issue briefly with Pearl in the hospital but hadn't really taken its consequences aboard, partly because she was young too, and there were no other zombies on the ward for the purposes of comparison. Given the points that Stan had been making about the benefits of exercise, though, it wasn't implausible that afterlife really might reawaken female appetites more effectively than HRT, and even conceivable that Marjorie Claridge's flirtatiousness wasn't entirely a matter of jest.

I even started thinking that Marjorie didn't look at all bad, for a late-forty-something albino, before I reminded myself, sternly, that I already had a girl-friend…or, at least, was truly and irredeemably in love.

CHAPTER SIX

When you really think about it—as you inevitably begin to do, once you've been raised from the dead—the most peculiar thing about afterlife status isn't the albinism at all, although that's the most obvious change. The most peculiar thing is something that doesn't change: the apparent age of the afterlifer. There's no logic to that, in my opinion. Superstimulant stem cells ought to rejuvenate as well as reanimating. Given that they're supposed to be restoring your body, they really ought to go all the way and do a thorough job.

Conspiracy theorists, inevitably, argue that it's all part of the plot, that it's a deliberate ploy on the part of the International Brotherhood of Freeburkers and a key element of their incomprehensible plot to take over the world by becoming the ultimate Masters of Life and Afterlife. According to that line of crazy thinking, the late-dying afterliving *could* be restored to their physical prime, just as one would expect from an authentic elixir of life, but the Burkers don't want that, firstly because it would make the afterliving young enough and virile enough to become a real fighting force, and secondly because it would enable them to breed. The second point, in the eyes of most conspiracy theorists, is critical. If the afterliving could have children, there really would be a possibility of them one day taking over the world and exterminating the living as a redundant nuisance. The age-freezing is thus seen as a side-effect or necessary corollary of sterilization. People who argue like that aren't fazed by the apparent fact that afterliving individuals who died young also seem to be sterile—they just assume that the Burkers take special measures in those cases.

If it really were the case that the freezing of apparent age during rebirth is a deliberate contrivance—in case you're in any doubt, it isn't—the ban on resurrecting children would be a further side-effect of a choice, rather than a corollary of an inconvenient necessity. Experiments showed way back in the 2020s that children even babies, *could* be resurrected using SSCs, just as easily as adults—but that they would then remain existentially becalmed indefinitely. Some Burkers, of course—with the plaintive support of numerous bereaved parents—wanted such resurrections to be licensed anyway, on the grounds that future science was sure to throw up technics that would allow the Peter Pans in question to resume growing up at a later date, but Parliament had refused to do that. After all, the bereaved parent vote wasn't very large, and the average age of MPs was way up in the fifties; they might have been in a hurry to get the legislation through, but they knew where their priorities lay.

Maybe prohibiting the resurrection of children was the right thing to do and maybe it wasn't—it's one of those issues that generates a lot of philosophical debate, even in pubs, let alone polite dinner parties—but the real mystery, as I said just now, is why the decision ever had to be made. Why don't SSCs rejuvenate as well as reanimate?

If they did, of course, they'd be as much use to the living as they are to the dead—everybody would want them, and Burkers wouldn't be Burkers but Basils, called after Basil Hallward, the artist who gifts Dorian Gray with potentially-eternal youth and beauty in Oscar Wilde's classic moral tale.

On the other hand, one has to consider the corollaries of rejuvenation seriously. Presumably, a brain that was rejuvenated rather than merely restored, would lost much of its accumulated knowledge and wisdom; the afterliving really would be very different people, freshly reborn—and so would the living who had to go back in time rather than simply being arrested in their progress. While not exactly a can of worms, possibilities like that wouldn't be entirely Utopian. If they offered humankind a bed of roses, it wouldn't be without its thorns.

But still the question remains: given that there is no vast Conspiracy of Mighty Burkers, isn't it weird that SSCs do what they do, in the way that they do it? If you ask me—not that anyone ever does, given that I only have a lousy English Lit degree and practically everybody else in the afterlife community thinks they know better than me because they're so old and they think I'm just a pretty face—it must be to do with gene-switching. The SSCs themselves are, of course, switch-free by definition, but the residual life they're working on, when they begin to resuscitate and mimic the cells of the individual they're resurrecting, they're operating on and taking their models from cells and tissues that have already reached a particular stage in the switching process: cells that already have their internal clocks set, in a way that can't be wound back.

That, I think, is why all the reborn start from where they left off in life, in terms of their apparent antiquity. It doesn't matter as much as you might imagine, though, because Stan Blake is absolutely right. Even Methuselahs can get fit—and they have every incentive to do so, once they're convinced that age is no longer taking a further toll…or taking it much more slowly than before.

One corollary of that, of course, is that even Methuselahs could make an army, if they wanted to.

Mercifully, they don't. I give you my word of honor on that. We are not a warlike kind.

* * * * * * *

By the time I'd been turning up to the Center for a week, the "physiotherapy" was getting to be the most enjoyable part of the day, so far as I was concerned. It only took me five days to become the only person in the squad who could actually last the full two hours along with Stan, and I flattered myself that I looked good doing it.

Stan was over the moon, if only because it gave him an excuse to carry on to the end himself. When I suggested to him that perhaps we might include some music that I liked along with *Highway to Hell* and *Shout at the Devil*, though, his immediate reaction was to frown.

"All in good time, Son," he said. "You're the new boy, remember—can't start throwing your weight around yet."

I decided that the *status quo* was tolerable, at least for a few weeks longer. It wasn't as if Stan didn't have standards. We did do *The Time Warp*, pretty much according to the instructions in the lyric, but were never called upon, even in jest, to resurrect *The Monster Mash*.

The practical advice sessions and counseling were less enjoyable, especially when the powers-that-be sent living hirelings in to do the advising. Nobody at the Center minded Andy Hazelhurst poking around, because we knew that he was just a self-seeking glory-grubber out for what he could get, and therefore had no interest at all in feeding us committee-produced bullshit, but everyone resented the script-followers who did nothing else.

I hated them even more than most, because their attitude and techniques reminded me strongly of my old job. Now that I was the one being soothed with weak encouragement and hollow pretence, I began to understand a little better how my own clients had felt about it. When I was mopping up after rockmobility on the last day of my first week, I confided to a couple of the others that I really wasn't looking forward to that afternoon's scheduled personal counselling session.

"You'll get used to it," Stan told me. "Just let it flow over you, like so much background noise. I know it's difficult, when they're trying to engage us all the time by asking questions, but it'll only take a fortnight or so for you to build up a repertoire of stock answers, so you won't have to engage your brain at all."

"But you need to keep that smart mouth of yours under control," Methuselah advised. "Don't piss them off—especially the retraining salesmen. They know as well as you do that it's all a farce, but they like to go through the motions without any fuss. Everybody benefits if it all goes smoothly. Sarcasm doesn't help."

I knew from long experience on the other side of the questionnaire that the Wise Old Man was right, although I couldn't help pointing out the irony that the only person at the Center who had a real job at present was Pearl, who was just as sarcastic as me.

"Yes," Andy Hazelhurst put in, having been eavesdropping on the conversation—it was difficult not to, given they layout of the tables and chairs—"but there's actually a demand for zombie nurses. Your chances of getting on to that particular retraining program, with your English Lit degree, are a bit slim."

"If you could get proper funding for your research," I retorted, "You could pay us a wage for serving as your guinea-pigs. That way we'd all have *proper jobs*. Even Methuselah."

"You have as much to gain from my investigations as I do, if not more," he told us, mimicking the patience of a saint. "Every discovery I make is of immediate relevance to you, and if I'm fortunate enough to make a significant one, it will have an immediate impact on your lives. You're volunteering in the best possible cause. You're the true knights of the living dead."

Nobody had laughed at that joke for years.

"What you ought to be doing," Jim Peel told the doctor, "is working flat out to find a way to give us back our skin color and allow us to pass for living…that would really rehabilitate us."

""No, Jim," Marjorie put in. "That's not the way to go about it. We shouldn't be trying to go into hiding, to conceal what we are. We should be trying to change social attitudes, to fight, not just for ourselves, but for justice."

"Just like you," Jim came back at her. "Except, of course, that you *are* in hiding, concealing who and where you are in your postings, whether you're ranting about zombie rights or the radical green agenda. I'll settle for the melanin."

Andy Hazelhurst hastened to pour oil on the briefly-troubled waters, or at least to deflect attention away from the immediate dispute with a little bluster. "Actually, he said, "that *is* one of the lines I'm working on, in the lab—but that kind of biochemical exploration only requires tissue-cultures, imagination and patience. I know that it must seem to you that all the measurements I take, and the little things I ask you do or swallow, are a bit pointless, but I have to be a trifle vague about what hypotheses I'm trying to test. We have to avoid the uncertainty principle, to the extent that's compatible with the principle of informed consent. If you know what results I'm expecting or aiming for, it's bound to affect the likelihood of their being produced. I give you as much explanation as I can, but you'll just have to take it on trust that I really am trying to produce results that will work to your benefit."

"As every anthropologist knows," Marjorie told him, mischievously "the only way to understand an alien culture is to go native. We'd be a lot more inclined to trust you if you were one of us. You're a doctor—you must have a hundred convenient ways of killing yourself ready to hand."

The doctor took the suggestion in good part, laughing even though it hadn't really been a joke. "Then I'd have to retrain," he said. "It would take at least two years to get back to where I am now, even if everything went smoothly. I can't afford to lose two years—it's a highly competitive field, you know." He always weathered such petty storms with ease, keeping his eye on the distant prize.

"What I think you should be working on," Methuselah put in, "is a way to give us dotards a bit more bodily strength and resilience. "It's all very well for Stan to bang on and on about how even eighty-year olds can keep fit, but I've been doing his accursed rockmobility for four years now, and all that practice hasn't given me the ability to do what young Nicky's been able to do within a week—stay the distance, that is. If you want to earn my undying gratitude, Andy, give me back my twenty-seven-year-old body. I'll try to live forever anyway, but I'd enjoy it a hell of a lot more...."

"Just give me time," the doctor said. "I'll do my best. Only hang on long enough, and you'll get your reward eventually."

"And rockmobility will help you hang on," Stan put in, "even if you can't stay the distance every morning."

"Would you want your twenty-seven-year-old brain back, though?" I asked him, having already given the matter some thought. "Would you want the memories and wisdom you acquired after that age to be wiped out?"

"That wouldn't be a necessary corollary," Methuselah said—although I couldn't see how he could be so sure about it. "My regenerated body obviously has a resilience that the old one lacked—adding in the appearance of youth would be a superficial thing, essentially cosmetic."

I had to leave the group broke up then, because my counsellor had arrived, but I survived the session without any undue stress on either side. She not only left convinced that I was perfectly sane, and adapting very well to my new condition, but that she had played some small part in that success herself—thus, no doubt, making her pathetic existence seem almost worthwhile, at least until she saw her next living client.

I sought out Methuselah again to tell him that I had followed his advice. He was sitting on his own; Andy Hazelhurst had gone, Stan was in conversation with Jim Peel on the far side of the room, and Marjorie was back on the workstations, pounding out yet another article.

"It was fine," I reported. "You and Stan are right—no point in worrying, just settle into the groove, keep my smart mouth zipped, and get it over with. I'm not looking forward to the retraining consultant on Monday, though. Whatever she wants to fix me up with, I know I'm not going to like it."

"Same principle," he said. "Go with the flow, and be polite. All you need is patience—you especially. You don't need rejuvenating to get the full benefit of our afterlife."

"Andy's right," I told him. "You'll get your full reward too, in time."

"Sure," he answered, plainly unconvinced. "When I look your age again, I'll give you a run for your money with young

Pearl. You might have to get a move on there, mind—now you're here to spur him on, Jim will be stepping up the pressure."

"I've already got a girl-friend," I told him.

"A living girl-friend?"

"Yes. We were practically engaged before…the bomb."

"It doesn't work that way," Methuselah assured me. "Living boys still chase zombie girls, because their raging hormones aren't fussy, and they're prone to all sorts of eccentric fetishism, but living girls won't have anything to do with zombie boys, even to piss off their parents."

"Isn't that a bit of an over-generalization?" I objected. "Not to mention blatantly sexist."

"Trust me, Son," he replied. "I may be old, but I know my birds and bees, and which is which, and I know the way the world works. Miss out on Pearl, and it might be quite some time before you get another chance. What's worse, the harpies will start to figure you for easy meat. Marjorie's all talk, but Alice… if she starts whispering in your ear about the advantages of making love to older women, make an excuse and leave."

I didn't believe him, of course, but the fact remained that Helena still wouldn't return my calls, now that I'd got a brand new pay-as-you-go phone, or reply to any emails I sent from home. I'd let her know my new details as soon as I'd got the account set up, ostensibly just for politeness' sake, but I'd also sent her a couple of other messages since then, tell her how much I missed her and asking her to get in touch. No joy so far.

He wasn't wrong about Alice, either. She had already engaged me in one suggestive conversation on the subject of the afterliving putting our obsolete prejudices aside, and adapting to the fact that the clocks of our existence had been restarted. She was a couple of years older than Marjorie, but equally well-preserved and far more feminine. I wasn't sure that I liked that, though. Alice didn't seem likely every to be able to appreciate my sense of humor, no matter how much practice she put in.

As I'd told Methuselah, though, and took care to inform Alice, I already had a girl-friend.

Methuselah's broad generalization did seem to have some truth in it, however; it wasn't just my older peers who openly courted Pearl—with little or no response. She had picked up a living stalker, who was often to be seen hanging around the Center.

"Did you know him when you were alive?" I asked her, one evening when she was hesitating at the window of the Center before heading back to the hospital accommodation-block where she lived.

"No," she said. "His mother's an out-patient at the hospital. He drives her in from the west Berks wilderness for dialysis twice a week. It's a sad case, actually—they're both under a lot of stress. He's quite harmless—embarrassing rather than dangerous."

"I thought stem cell treatments had virtually put an end to the need for dialysis," I said.

"Not entirely. Most defective kidneys can be repaired that way, but Timmy's mother has the most awkward kind. Her kidneys are in the front line of a variety of lupus that's gradually ruining all her organs. Stem cells can't fight it because it's an auto-immune disease, so the stem-cells come under attack as soon as they go to work."

"What about alternative treatments?"

"The dialysis *is* the alternative, although it's just a stopgap. Poor Timmy wanted us to transplant one of his kidneys, but we had to explain to him that, precisely because he's a compatible match, the auto-immune disease would attack the transplanted kidney too. The worst of it is that she's not a candidate for resurrection. Even SSCs can't defeat this particular enemy. She's relentlessly cheerful about it—she belongs to the County Set. You know the type: upper-middle class with aristocratic pretensions, takes the view that no miserable disease has any right to kill her. She puts on an act of being convinced that she only has to stay positive and she'll pull through, but I doubt that she really believes it, and Timmy certainly knows that the fact that his father is a gentleman farmer with a second home in the Highlands doesn't make a damn of difference to the fact that Mummy's doomed. You can understand why he's not quite himself, given that he's the one who has to look after her while Daddy's busy fighting the Depression. Getting fixated on me is just a displacement of his true feelings, and it really isn't any inconvenience to me that he drives his silly little car all the way to Reading even when his mother doesn't have an appointment, so he can follow me around."

"I don't know," I said, dubiously. "People like that can sometimes seem harmless, and then suddenly explode…."

"Not Timmy," she insisted. "I'm not afraid of him. There's no need."

"I'll walk you home, Pearl," Jim Peel was quick to volunteer, having overheard what she'd said and instantly taken the inference that she meant the opposite of what she'd said. "He won't dare mess with me."

I assumed that he was right about that; resurrection had restored every lumpen inch of his massive frame, and six months of rockmobility—of which he rarely survived more than half an hour at a time—had not yet made much of a dent on his brickshithouse build.

"He wouldn't dare mess with me, either," Pearl retorted, sharply. "He's just an embarrassment, okay? I'm more worried about him than me. If he gets tagged as a zombie-fancier, he's more likely to get roughed up than I am."

"And nobody's likely to be intimidated by him, in spite of his name," I couldn't resist putting in. Nobody smiled.

"Even so," Jim persisted, "you oughtn't to walk back alone at this time of night. It's midsummer, I know, but it's still late—and once the nights start drawing in again, you'll certainly need an escort."

"Don't be stupid," she said. "If we start going out in gangs, anticipating trouble, it won't be long before we get it—and if you start using those football-sized fists, no matter what the provocation is, you'll give the anti-resurrection brigade exactly what they're gagging for: a violent zombie. It's not your fault that you could pass for King Kong in a dim light, but it does mean that you have to be extra careful."

"So your plan is to let any crazy demon-slayer or kinky rapist you come across just get on with it?" Jim countered.

"Sure. The cause needs victims, not aggressors—and I've already committed suicide once, remember."

Jim had no answer to that, but he wasn't happy about it. "I'm right, you know," he said to me, when Pearl had left and we were about to go our own separate ways to our respective homes. "When the nights start drawing in again, things will get worse. Every year changes the balance, because there are more of us, and the novelty's wearing off. The ED have other targets in their sights, so hating us is still a sideline for them, but they're not the only crazy vigilantes in town. We need to prepare for the worst, my friend. It might not come this year, or next, but it will come."

Personally, I thought he'd be much better off trying to find or found a zombie rugby club than planning civil defense strategies, but I didn't dare say so while I was still the new boy. I went home instead, hoping to spent a quiet hour or two watching TV in that comfortable golden silence families develop when they've run out of things to say, or the need to say anything at all.

Alas, that was something else I'd lost along with life. Even Dad felt obliged to talk, simply because he was afraid of what silence might imply.

CHAPTER SEVEN

Is it inevitable that war will eventually break out between the living and the afterliving? Not many people of either kind think that it will happen soon—most think that it won't happen in your lifetime, and maybe not in my afterlifetime—but there are plenty of people on both sides of the Great Existential Divide who are prepared to shrug their shoulders and contend that there will, ultimately, come a day....

To some, it's a simple matter of statistics. If the zombie population continues to increase in proportion to the population of the living—as it surely will, unless the unfolding ecocatastrophe precipitates a scenario in which resurrection is prohibited or its supporting technics are lost—then the day will eventually come when the afterliving threaten to become a majority, capable by democratic authority or sheer brute force of taking the reins of regulation. Unwilling to surrender that power, the argument holds, the living will take every possible action to preserve it... up to and including warfare.

In a war of extermination, who would win? The general assumption is that it would be the living, because they currently hold the reins of power and possess all the guns. The afterliving are, in essence, only present in the world on their sufferance, under their license. Living people arguing along those lines almost invariably point out that, if the living really are bound to feel forced to exterminate the afterliving some day, then it might be as well to do it sooner rather than later, before too much power and too many guns leak away to the other side.

Living people with a less bellicose turn of mind point out that if a war of extermination is inevitable, the simplest thing to do is to stop resurrecting people—a practise that is, at present, almost entirely under the control of the living—either right now or in the not-too-distant future.

The Utopians among us, of course, argue that the matter can be settled peacefully: that the only thing we rally have to fear is fear itself—which is to say, the possibility that, if the living allow themselves to become convinced that war is inevitable, then, and only then, it will become inevitable. If we can only conquer fear, the Utopians contend, then negotiation can and will permit the eventual establishment of a stable, artificially-maintained ratio of the living and afterliving, within a total human population that will, of necessity, have to be stabilized and artificially-maintained in any case. Within that context, the Utopians argue, the human rights of the living and the afterliving can and will be maintained to the benefit of both parties.

To which the dystopian opposition generally replies: "Good luck with that!" and nods in the direction of past history.

Even the Utopian argument tends to leave unsettled the question of what the ideal artificially-maintained ratio might be, as a matter for future negotiation. Would the numbers have to be equal to eliminate resentment? Would resentment be eliminated even if they were? How would it affect the issue of the longevity of the living were to be significantly increased by ever-smarter stem cells, perhaps to the point of emortality? Would that make ultimate war more or less likely?

What do I think? I have to confess that I really don't know.

On the whole, and for the time being, I'm inclined to adopt a pragmatist stance. Even if war is inevitable, then let's do everything humanly possible to postpone it for as long as we can. Let's just try to keep the lid on, today, next week, next year... and for as long as we might live and afterlive. Isn't that what we're presently doing, in order to stave off the ecocatastrophe that will put an end of the present world economic system? And hasn't it worked, at least thus far, and for considerably longer than anyone could have anticipated twenty years ago? The world economic system probably can't last an afterlifetime, even if it contrives to increase its rate of evolution, but resurrection technics are still improving at an unsteady but relentless pace, so change isn't likely to stop any time soon. And if change is inevitable, what can we do except take a pragmatic point of view, and try to ride the tidal wave as best we can?

At the end of the day, it's the crucial but as-yet-undetermined data that will determine the limits of the possible and the politically practicable. We already know that the living and afterliving alike can be permanently destroyed, and we know that a second lease of afterlife is currently harder to obtain than the first, but nobody knows whether afterlifers really are potentially capable of afterliving forever, in the absence of violent destruction...and nobody knows, either, whether the living might acquire a similar prerogative tomorrow, next year or a hundred years hence.

While we don't know things like that, wouldn't we be criminally foolish to rush to any kind of Armageddon?

Even if it turns out that the afterliving aren't as long-lived as we hope, and that the living won't acquire the ability to cheat death for a long time yet, there remains one major factor on the Utopian side of the argument, and one major reason why the living would be imbeciles to ban resurrection any time soon, let alone start a war against the afterliving. Thus far, and until there's a major breakthrough in living medicine, the best hope the living have of *any* kind of further existence, let alone of any real measure of longevity on a Methuselahesque scale, is to die in the right place, at the right time, in a judicious manner.

* * * * * * *

Dad wasn't just intent on talking, he was also in a slightly cantankerous mood. "What do they think up at the Center about this Jarndyce business?" he wanted to know.

"I haven't taken a poll," I said, "and it's not exactly a hot topic of observation either side of rockmobility, but I think the general consensus is that we'd rather he stayed dead."

"Really?" he said, as if that were cause for surprise. "I thought your lot would be up in arms, protesting against the assumption that just because the living man's a homicidal maniac preying on innocent children, his zombie version would have the same tendencies."

"Not that I've noticed," I told him, generously overlooking his use of the terms *your lot* and *zombie*. "On the whole, I think most of us tend to the opinion that we'd rather not take the risk."

"In case he started murdering zombies—or whatever it is that a zombicidal maniac would be doing if we can't call it murder?"

It didn't seem diplomatic, or particularly relevant, to point out that an afterliving paedophile wouldn't have any opportunity to manifest his predilections within his own community, as yet. "In case he were to resume killing *anyone*," I actually replied, as mildly as I could. "I know it's a touchy question, with all the sticky issues of human rights, social discrimination and all, but, at the end of the day, I think most people would rather not see resurrection employed to complicate and perpetuate problems that we still find intractable in life."

"So zombies are in favor of selection—they want to be able to exercise control over who joins their ranks, on other grounds than medical feasibility?"

"Jesus, Dad," I said. "I can't speak for the afterliving any more than you can speak for the living—and the simple fact is that we don't and can't control the Burkers' selection policies. That's a matter for the law and their own Ethics Committees."

Stupid name, Burkers," was his reply to that. "Where does it come from, anyway?" Evidently, no one had told him about Burke and Hare, the archetypal Resurrection Men.

"It's from Edmund Burke," I told him, earnestly. "The man who wrote a classic essay on the aesthetics of the sublime. It's because their work is essentially sublime and transcendent—a crucial enhancement of the human condition."

I didn't mention Burke's contention that the sublime always

had an element of horror in it, even though I knew about it. It was because I'd done English Lit at university that I'd ended up in the Civil Service rather than some line of work that might qualify as "wealth-creating," and that was still a slightly sore point with Dad, who'd rather I'd gone into business, and would probably have settled for Burking in a pinch.

Except, of course, that I handed "ended up" in the Civil Service at all. I'd almost certainly have to change career, now that my application to rejoin the Great Bureaucratic Army had been rejected—or, as the letter from the OO had actually put it "held in suspension until a suitable appointment becomes available." Nowadays, no one ever gets turned down; they merely get placed in a potentially-endless queue; it makes legal redress so much harder to obtain.

"That's ridiculous," Dad said, perceptively—but at least he took the hint and dropped the discussion…and didn't pick it up the following day, being prepared for once in his life actually to let the Sabbath function as a day of rest.

On Monday, after rockmobility, I submitted meekly to my appointment to discuss my reconfigured career prospects with my employment counsellor, who visited the Center for that purpose. She was very sympathetic, of course; that was in her script. She was younger than me, so I knew that she wasn't long out of training, and that the script would be fresh in her mind.

"I can understand why you want to maintain career continuity, Mr. Rosewell," she assured me, "but the fact is that the Ombudman's Office isn't really in a position to recruit just now. The government is attempting to revise the whole system of handling grievances, and while you might eventually be able to obtain an appointment in whatever administrative structure replaces the OO, that's not likely to happen for some time. Even if you hadn't had your…accident, it might have been high time to think about retraining."

"It wasn't an accident," I pointed out, mildly. "I was murdered. Cruelly slain while hurrying back to work after my lunch-break, in order to fulfil my duty to Crown and Country."

"Unfortunately," she continued, unfazed, "the five years of experience you accumulated in the OO aren't really sufficient to place you in a competitive situation, at a time when there are a great many displaced civil servants jockeying for a relatively limited number of new situations, and your educational qualifications are rather devoid of *vocational components*. Nothing very *practical*, or even *mathematical*."

"I did the scientific component of the bac," I pointed out. "It's compulsory."

"For which reason, everyone else of a similar age has done it too," she countered. "Your scores are good, admittedly, but not *that* good, considering the intense competitiveness of the current employment environment. Given your literacy levels, it might be better to think in terms of something along the lines of web content provision."

"I thought all that sort of work had been subcontracted to India—which is, I guess, where the substitute for the Ombudsman's Office is likely to end up."

"It is the sort of field in which competition is effectively global," she admitted, with a slight and presumably-unscripted sigh.

"It's not as bad as all that, though," I told her, blandly. "Think how much worse it would be if the Americans and Australians were functionally literate. As things stand, the British rank second only to the Dutch when it comes to competence in the English language, so if anyone can compete with the Indians, it's us…though not, alas, on the cost of labor."

She didn't formulate the ghost of a laugh. It wasn't surprising—the joke about the Dutch was *very* old, and I'd been very careful to maintain the earnestness of my facial expression. Not that she would have noticed, given the lengths to which she was going in order to avoid eye contact. Pink obviously wasn't her favourite color.

"As it happens," she told me, "there *is* a training program in web content provision for which I can sign you up. All home study, two months' duration if you pass all the stages at the first attempt. There's no guarantee of a job at the end of it, I'm afraid, but it will add an extra string to your bow."

I already knew that several of the regulars at the Center, including Stan Blake, had gone through half a dozen such home-study programs already, and now had enough strings to their bow to call it a guitar and play *Smoke on the Water*—but no actual job. I also knew that I had to accept the offer, because participation in the program offered a small increase in my dole, and the threat of a cut if I refused.

"I'll be happy to give it a try," I assured her, knowing that there was a sequence of tick-boxes on her digipad where she had to pass judgment on my attitude. I'd had some fun with those tick-boxes in my time, and I'd cut it rather fine with the marginally flippant remarks I'd already made.

"That's good," she said. "I'll email all the forms, and you can start tomorrow. Will you be using the workstations here?"

"No," I said. "I'm one of the rare zombies who still has a home of sorts, in the bosom of his family."

Mercifully, she didn't say: "Good luck with that."

As chance would have it, my "literacy skills" had already found a demand of sorts within the Center, where the workstations were in more-or-less continuous use, and not just for government-sponsored training schemes. At least three of the old guard, including Methuselah, were busy writing their autobiographies, and at least three of the intermediate generation were getting heavily into zombie rights e-forums. Once the rumor had got around that I was more reliable than mechanical spellcheckers and grammar-checkers, I'd been appointed the Center's volunteer proofreader-in-chief.

"I know it's rather boring," Methuselah told me, when I'd looked over his latest chapter later that afternoon, "but it's an important project nevertheless. The afterliving are, after all, the only people properly qualified to write autobiographies—not only because their lives are complete but because their point of view is, if not absolutely objective, at least definitively external." He really did talk like that—you can imagine how he wrote, and why he was in need of a proofreader. On the other hand, I could see distinct similarities between his writing style and my own...which, I suppose, only increased my value as an editorial adviser.

"I can see your point," I conceded.

"Then again," he said, "it might turn out to be an invaluable exercise from the personal point of view. Whether or not, and to what extent, I'm a different person now from the one I used to be, I'll certainly become increasingly distanced from him as time goes by. If I don't record my impressions of my living self now, in as much detail as I can, I might lose part or all of it. You should write your life story too, you know, even though you died so young...especially because you died so young. You don't want to lose touch with the person you once were."

"If he was actually anyone at all," I said. "He'd been a trifle lazy, I fear—he always thought of achievement as something he'd have time for later. Still does, alas." *Except that he had figured out who he wanted to do it with*, I added silently, for my own benefit. *And still does, alas.*

"Pearl's writing her autobiography," Methuselah observed, politely refraining from protesting against my self-denigration.

"Is she?" I said. "She hasn't asked me to proofread it. She probably thinks that her English is every bit as good as mine."

"Probably," Methuselah agreed, probably implying that he had another possibility in mind. It was probably the same one that had occurred to me: that Pearl might not want her fellow zombies reading her account of why she'd killed herself—assuming that she had figured it out herself.

"What about Stan?" I asked. "Nobody seems to know much about his lifetime."

"He doesn't seem to be much inclined toward writing—more a man of action."

"And Marjorie? As you pointed out to me when I met you on my first day, she's the only one among us who was actually famous, to some degree, while she was alive. She's certainly inclined toward writing."

"Far too busy," Methuselah said, shaking his head slowly. "Still trying to change the world—for the better, mercifully."

At that moment, one of the panes in the windows in the front of the building shattered, and a pebble whizzed through, landing on top of the table at which we were sitting. Fortunately, the broken glass didn't carry that far.

"Fuck!" howled Stan, and bounded to the door.

He'd only been outside for a few seconds, though, before he came back in. "Bloody kids!" he said.

In all fairness, I thought, it must have been a very well-aimed stone, or a lucky one, because both of the windows at the front were protected outside by stout iron bars that were not so very far apart. Most stones hurled at the windows bounced back, or at least took a deflection before colliding with a pane or part of the wooden frame. The glass in the panes wasn't bullet-proof, but it was quite strong, and required a direct hit at considerable velocity to break it.

I walked over to where the stone had landed, near the door to the kitchenette, and picked it up.

"At least it hasn't got a piece of paper wrapped round it inscribed with a black spot," I said, trying to make light of the matter.

"We've already had our ration of black spots," Stan told me, still seething. "If it were up to me, I'd just put steel shutters over the damned windows. After all, we don't need the daylight, do we?"

"It's probably a good idea not to make the place look like a bunker," Methuselah told him, as he fetched a broom in order to sweep up the broken glass. "Anyway, its Council property. It's up to them to replace it."

"Sure it is," Stan said. "If I don't do it myself, it'll take them at least three weeks—and it won't do a bit of good to send them the invoice. They'll just sent it back stamped UNAPPROVED."

"At least it's midsummer," I said. "The draught won't be icy."

"And at least they ran away," Marjorie put in. "It'll be time to worry when they wait for you to come out of the door and start pelting *you*."

"It's only a matter of time," Jim Peel opined. He was standing at the window, fearlessly looking out, as if to threaten any other potential stone-throwers with the bulk of his presence—or provide them with a tempting target. No one took up the challenge, thank God. "Your stalker's out there again," he said to Pearl. "Tonight, you really must let me walk you back to the hospital."

"I'll go talk to him," Pearl said. She got up from her armchair and headed for the door.

Stan intercepted her. "I really don't think that's a good idea, Pearl," he said.

"Why? You surely don't think it was him who threw the stone?"

"No, of course not—but you've said yourself that it wouldn't be a good idea to identify him as a zombie-lover to anyone else who might be watching the building. While he's out there on his own, he's just an idler, but if you engage him in conversation...."

"*Are* there people watching the building?" I asked.

"Probably," Stan said. "Even if they're only curtain-twitchers, gossip will spread. Best leave him alone, love."

It was probably the only argument that could have made Pearl change her mind, but it worked. She sat down again. "He is harmless, though," she insisted. "He's just having a hard time, that's all."

"Nobody doubts that your heart's in the right place," Stan told her. "We just worry about you."

"Nobody here," she muttered.

As I was still standing up, and Metrhuselah was still busy picking up bits of broken glass, it didn't seem inappropriate to sit down next to her for a minute or two. "Somebody at the hospital giving you a hard time?" I asked.

She shrugged. "Nothing serious, You've been there—you know what it's like."

"Not the idiot with the crossed index-fingers?"

"He's not the only one. We don't have anyone newly passed over on the wards just now, so I'm working entirely with the living, and some of them can be difficult. It's not their fault, mind—they're in hospital, after all, hurting and scared. They turn their anxiety wherever they can, just to get it away from themselves for a moment or two. The living nurses take flak too. It comes with the territory."

"Can I walk you home, then?" I asked.

"No," she said. "You've got a girl-friend, remember? I met her when she came to see what had become of you."

I really didn't see how that was relevant, but I let it pass. I didn't want to start a row—and I didn't want to annoy Jim Peel any more than I just had, by substituting my offer for his.

I went back to my former position, to resume pointing out the errors of Methuselah's grammatical ways.

CHAPTER EIGHT

I'd been warned more than once about the possibility that my appetites might change, so I was rather disappointed that they didn't, much. On the other hand, I'd always been a meat-and-two-veg kind of person, having inherited the habit from Dad *via* Mum, so the two major shifts associated with conversion by anecdotal evidence—a keener appetite for meat and a marked distaste for highly-spiced food—didn't really apply to me.

It's possible, of course, that the former shift is all in the mind—not just the minds of zombies but those of their living observers. When you borrow a word like "zombie" from the lexicon of the folkloristic and cinematic imagination to apply to an actual but novel phenomenon, there's bound to be a certain amount of mythical pollution. Because the zombies of modern legend were supposed to be driven by cannibalistic appetites, it was only natural that some such suspicion should fall on the actual beneficiaries of medical resurrection, if not in any serious sense, at least in jest. Nor is it surprising that the suspicion should be carefully toned down to credible proportions. The living must have been pre-inclined to look for evidence of enhanced carnivorism in the afterliving, and the afterliving must have been be pre-inclined to look for it in themselves. A rapid proliferation of supportive anecdotes was only to be expected.

The second element of allegation is, however, less expectable, especially in view of the common analogy drawn between supposed "zombie cravings" and those of pregnant women. Pregnant women are routinely said to develop cravings *for* highly-spiced foods, not aversions to them. It is, however, conceivable that what was involved here, in the semi-conscious processes of rumor-mongering, was a deliberate inversion. The one thing that differentiates afterliving females most conspicuously from living ones—far more conspicuously than mere paleness of complexion—is that afterliving women do not, so far as anyone can yet tell, fall pregnant. They are, in a sense, not merely a pale shadow but an antithesis of their living counterparts: hence, in pseudological terms, the inversion of their craving.

Having said all that, though, I must confess that I did become noticeably hungrier than I had been in life. If my appetite didn't change in direction, it did in volume. Whether that had anything to do with physiological changes in my ability to process the various major food-groups, I don't know, but I was more inclined to put it down to enthusiastic rockmobility. I'd had a reasonable amount of exercise while I was alive, at least during the football season, but the "training" we'd done for the Sunday Morning League was nowhere near as intensive as Stan's daily workouts. The fact that I'd rapidly made it a point of pride to finish the scheduled two hours—because rather than in spite of the fact that no one else seemed able to do it—meant that I was throwing myself into it more wholeheartedly than I'd ever thrown myself into *anything* in life.

Mum obviously noticed my enhanced appetite, and started increasing my portions without being asked, but she didn't comment on it, almost as if she was afraid to bring it out into the open. I tried to open the subject by offering to increase the housekeeping money I was giving her from my dole, but she refused. If Dad noticed, he didn't comment. Kirsten probably did, but she was always on a diet anyway, and knew better than to comment on what anyone else was eating in case she became the butt of retaliatory mockery. If it had been practical, I would have eaten more at lunch-time, when I as usually at the Center, but ordering food to be delivered there was far more expensive, and I simply didn't have the money.

I comforted myself by telling myself that it wouldn't be surprising if all zombies had to eat more than the living, simply because they had a different kind of life to support—and that it wouldn't be surprising, either, if they mostly kept quiet about it, for fear of being stigmatized as even more of a burden on the world's dwindling resources than they constituted simply by virtue of existing.

That was the way I was beginning to think, when my philosophical moods gripped me.

* * * * * * *

On my way to the Center on the Wednesday of that week I had my first run-in with religious nuts. I suppose I should have been ready for it, but I wasn't. The nuts in question were Afro-Anglicans, although I didn't attack any particular significance to the denomination. I couldn't tell whether they were from Nigeria, Kenya, Zimbabwe or some less prolific source of the inspired, but I knew they weren't regulars at the local Anderson Baptist Church round the corner from where my parents lived, which seemed to be attended entirely by middle-aged Jamaican ladies who'd known me by sight when I was in short trousers and still occasionally said hello to me on Sunday mornings without giving the slightest sign that they'd noticed that I'd turned into a zombie.

The nuts were lurking in wait for me round the corner of London Road. Obviously, the news had got around that my daily routine involved walking to the Center on my own, at more-or-les the same time, most days of the week. There were three of them, although two of them were obviously only there to lend crude but effective support to the would-be exorcist, which they did by flanking him like a pair of flying buttresses.

When the exorcist—who might actually have been an ordained minister, for all I know—launched into his spiel, I briefly considered pushing past and proceeding on my way, but I figured that they'd only follow me, so I thought, after careful and rational consideration, that it would be best to stand my ground and brazen it out stoically, putting on a saintly display of patience and tolerance.

Only joking. Actually, I guess I panicked. At any rate, I lost my rag.

If the guy who was trying to send me straight to hell without passing *go* had been chanting in Latin I'd have understood at least a few words and might even have been able to correct some of his grammar, but whatever Missal he was holding was printed in some language with which I was totally unfamiliar. If I'd been able to see the humor of it, I might have been able to laugh the whole thing off, but I wasn't in a laughing mood, and I let that show.

"Come on, you freaks," I said, raising my voice so that the dawdling passers-by would get the full benefit. "I see the book, but I don't see the bell or the candle. There are three of you, for God's sake—surely you could manage a bell and a candle between you. If you're going to play the part, at least try to get it right. Mind you, it's a pretty lousy part, isn't it? I mean, all the world's a stage, so we have no choice but to play our roles, but at least we get to be our own casting directors and script-writers. What kind of brain-dead backwoodsman, given the choice, would actually volunteer to become a missionary, dispatched from his gloriously Godforsaken equatorial backwater to make a pathetic attempt to re-convert the heathen descendants of the cack-handed imperialist scum who forced his great-great-great grandfather to give up his own perfectly adequate mumbo-jumbo in favour of the whiter-than-white brand? Obviously, you're no good at football or you'd be representing Manchester or Birmingham in the Premier League, but is there really no other option but lurk on street-corners, like flashers in Oxfam-bought macs, waiting for some poor sod you can fail to persecute with a ludicrously fake exorcism that couldn't even send a hungry cockroach scuttling back behind the fridge. Give me a fucking break, why don't you?"

It was at that point that I realized that I was shouting, not only drowning out the sound of the attempted exorcism by making myself clearly audible on the other side of the road, spite of the roar of the traffic. At least thirty people had stopped to stare, at distances ranging from ten feet to thirty yards, and at least half of those had their mobile phones out, filming every last word and gesture. I knew that the video would have been posted at half a dozen different locations on the web by the time I reached the Center, and suddenly had a moment of terrible doubt, wondering what the hell my casting director could have been thinking, and wishing that my script-writer had done a considerably more measured and better proof-read job.

"On the other hand," I continued, in a more measured voice. "Why not? Just go ahead, why don't you? Why should I care whether you send me to hell or not? What have I got to lose?" *My girl-friend isn't even speaking to me*, I didn't add. When you're being filmed, you have to be careful not to give in to self-pity, because it's the least photogenic emotion there is.

When the Afro-Anglican preacher finished, he actually looked surprised that I was still there, although I couldn't believe, even for an instant, that he'd actually thought I was going to disappear infernowards.

"Oh my," I said, struggling to keep my voice strictly on the level and as mild as milk. "I feel just terrible—as if archangels with flaming swords were slicing and dicing me. Oh, the agony. Oh, the awesome revelation. Oh, the cringe-making power of the Great Almighty. Oh dear, look at the time—must be off, lads. Same time tomorrow? No? I expect you've got other demons to hunt down. Busy, busy, busy—no rest for the unwicked. Here endeth the lesson for today. Amen."

I didn't try to excavate a path between the pillar of the church and one of the flying buttresses; I walked around the entire party. They didn't follow me. Neither did the crowd of amateur cameramen, who were rooted to the spot by the need to email their little windfall.

I couldn't help wondering what Wise Old Methuselah would think if and when he happened to pick up the performance, or even Stan the action man, let alone Dad or Helena. None of them, I felt certain, would be amused. I tried to take refuse in the thought that *Kirsten*, at least, would be able to laugh at it, even though I hadn't been at my best—but I couldn't convince myself even of that.

I knew that it was no good hoping that everyone would miss it; any selectorbot programmed to pick up local news would flag it. By the time we'd finished rockmobility, if not before, every workstation at the Sally Ann would be flashing alerts to every user who sat down there.

Surely, I thought, Marjorie Claridge would understand and sympathize.

If she did, she didn't say anything. The most surprising thing of all, perhaps, was that nobody actually *said* anything. By lunch-time, they must all have seen and heard it, and must have known that I knew that they knew, but they didn't utter a word of criticism—not directly or explicitly, at any rate.

I was a newreborn. They were making allowances. And they *did* understand…and, at least after a fashion, sympathize.

That afternoon, Marjorie asked me if I'd take a look at her latest brief epic before she posted it. I knew that she didn't think that she needed a proof-reader, so my first thought was that she was just trying, in her subtle fashion, to let me know how protest *ought* to be carried out, soberly, carefully and decorously.

Once I'd read what she had written, though, that hypothesis didn't seem quite so plausible.

"I realize that you'll be posting this anonymously," I said, "but wouldn't it be better to tone it down a bit? I understand that you're only extrapolating a philosophical argument, but there are sentences in here that, if taken out of context, might seem to be breaking the law, let alone stirring up trouble."

"Law?" she said. "What law do you mean?"

"The law prohibiting public incitement to violence."

"Is there one?" she said, with blatant disingenuity. "And even if there is, how could a rational philosophical argument be held to be breaking it?"

"Well," I said, trying to choose my words carefully, "even though you don't quite say so in so many words, some people might think that what you're advocating here is that the afterliving should be allowed, in certain circumstances, to murder the living, in order to increase their own numbers proportionately."

"Nonsense," she retorted. "What I'm arguing, purely hypothetically, is that if the afterliving have the same human rights as other members of the human population, as they surely should under any conceivable system of justice, then that includes the right of reproduction. Given that there's only one way, at present, that the afterliving can reproduce, the logic of the argument suggests that the conversion of a living person should be regarded as a rightful act, provided that the principle of informed consent is observed. You've only been here a matter of days, and you're obviously unfamiliar with the earlier articles in the series, but if you'd been following it, you'd have seen that I've already demolished the moral case for continuing to regard calculated and mutually-agreed acts of conversion as homicidal, so I might seem to you to be taking a little too much for granted, but...."

"Well, maybe," I agreed, "but it seems to me that your rhetoric does occasionally go beyond what might be considered typical of a balanced philosophical argument...."

"*Balanced!*" she interjected. "Balance is for wimps who refuse to reach conclusions. There's no *balance* in logic. A conclusion is either true or it isn't. Mine is. The afterliving not only have a moral entitlement to help the living pass over, but a moral obligation, in instances where inaction would permit further organic deterioration to a state in which resurrection would be impossible, or even unlikely. You were fortunate enough never to grow old, but have you the slightest idea how many people there are in Britain whose chances of resurrection are diminishing and vanishing with every passing day? Tens of thousands...hundreds of thousands...millions. If we aren't prepared to help them, who is? Not their living brethren, that's for sure!"

"Well, maybe," I agreed, again, "but if you look at it that way, there isn't actually anyone over the age of eighteen currently alive whose chances of resurrection are increasing on a daily basis, are there? So where do you draw the line?"

"*Exactly!*" she exclaimed, emphatically. "I knew you'd understand, Nicky. That's exactly what this whole discussion is about—and exactly what *you* should be thinking about, instead of bouncing about to *Shout at the Devil* or mooning after young Pearl. Where should the lines be drawn?—not just thus one, but all the others. My *next* article will be about infantile resurrection—and it'll come out strongly in favor. To be perfectly frank, I won't care overmuch what you or anybody else thinks about that one, either, but I'll give it to you to read anyway."

As nobody else was mentioning it, I thought it was time I did. "This is about this morning, isn't it? It's your way of ticking me off about making an exhibition of myself, by forcing me to be critical of public recklessness. You're not really going to post this at all, are you?"

She seemed genuinely surprised. "You really haven't read my earlier stuff, have you? Not that it would get flagged on your machine, of course, since it's an anonymous. Of course I'm going to post it—and any fool who cares to misconstrue it as an incitement to murder is welcome to do so, in the interests of heating up the debate. But yes, Nicky, if you're going pitch in with the lunatic fringe, you do need to plan what you're going to do. Stan and Methuselah might advise you to tone it down, but all you'll ever get from me is 'Go for it!' As I said, balance is for wimps, and boundaries too—but you do need to know what you're getting into. If that's who you are, good, but make sure you're doing it deliberately, and not just exploding at random. Leave that to the suicide bombers."

I didn't know what else to say, so I contented myself with pointing out a few errors in punctuation in her article, just in case she wanted to correct them.

When she returned to her workstation, leaving me alone, I

wondered how her article on infant resurrection was going to argue the case in favor. I was looking forward to it already. *So what if resurrected children get stuck at the age of six, or even six months, for an indefinite period?* I ventured, hypothetically. *Wouldn't most parents prefer that? How many parents* really *want their kids to grow up, and grow away from them, to reach the inevitable conclusion that their Mummy isn't a cornucopia of unlimited love and that Daddy isn't God's right hand man. Why not give people what they* really *want: the spontaneous and wholehearted affection of their unwitting little darlings, for ever and ever?*

To be fair to Marjorie, though, I had to admit that infantile resurrection was an important philosophical test case, and did need thrashing out. If it were considered immoral to use resurrection technology in certain cases—and beyond infantile resurrection there was the question of fetal resurrection—exactly where *was* it reasonable to draw the line…and if the use of resurrectionist technology were to be considered immoral in some instances, what became of the argument that anyone capable of resurrection had a moral right to its employment, as Blaise Jarndyce's lawyers were currently arguing before the High Court?

Methuselah came to check up on me before I'd taken the silent argument any further.

"Are you all right, Son?" he asked.

"Fine," I assured him.

"Was Marjorie telling you off?"

"Actually, no," I said. "She was just chatting, as one amateur philosopher to another, employing the Socratic method in order to inch me a little bit closer to the age of reason."

He might not have understood exactly what I meant, but he got the gist. "You do know that she was murdered, don't you?" he said. "Probably because she got to be a nuisance while she was campaigning for Greenpeace."

"I know," I said. "My sister tipped me off, so I looked it up. Killed in a hit-and-run that wasn't an accident. They never identified the vehicle or the driver. Conspiracy theories abound, MI5 and Big Oil being the favorite finger-pointing targets. I haven't tried to talk to her about it, though—I'm not sure how touchy the subject is."

"Marjorie doesn't believe in touchy subjects. For a while, she was careful, but there was no way she was going to be kept down for long. Even so, it might be a good idea if you didn't egg her on."

"Me?" I said. "Egg *her* on? I'm just a newreborn. She's not going to take any notice of me, is she?"

"Maybe not—but she does seem to like you. She seems to feel that you and she have something in common, maybe because you were murdered too."

"And you think I might be setting her a *bad example?* You think I might be in danger of *leading her astray?*"

"All I'm saying," Methuselah continued, patiently, "is that you need to be careful where Marjorie's concerned. She's vulnerable, in more ways than one."

It was Jim Peel's turn next. He sat down in the chair that Methuselah had vacated like a sack of coal falling off a lorry. "Okay, Mate?" he said.

"Sure," I replied.

"Maybe you and I ought to go out some evening and throw a ball around—or even kick one, if you're really committed to the round variety. Make a change from rockmobility, wouldn't it? I really miss it, you know. Not that I've given up, but the team I used to play for have had to put me on a reserve list while they get an eligibility ruling from the Union."

"Mine too," I said. "What a coincidence."

"Just between you and me," he said, "I don't think they're going to get it sorted before the season starts."

"Nor do I."

"So," he said, "we might have to think about some sort of arrangement of our own. I've talked about it to Stan, and Kevin….we might have to compromise on exactly what kind of ball we kick around, but in principle…well, there's no reason why we shouldn't do something. Something *outside*, I mean. In the evenings, when the sun's not so bright."

"No reason at all," I agreed.

When he'd gone, Stan inevitably took his place.

"Jim talking to you about outdoor games, was he?" he said.

I nodded. "He says you're up for it," I commented.

"He also says that his rugby club have out him on a reserve list—and he's got at last a dozen job applications held in suspension awaiting a favourable opportunity to arise. Not the done thing to say *no* to anyone nowadays, is it?"

"Except behind their backs, of course," I observed. "Why shouldn't we play out, Stan? We're old enough, aren't we?"

"No reason at all," he said, refusing to take offense, "if we can solve the practical problems. But you can see the practical problems, can't you, Nicky?"

"Oh yes," I agreed. "Can't walk down the street without tripping over them. Got to be careful, haven't we? Delicate skin and all that."

"I knew you'd understand," he said, apparently satisfied. "You're a smart boy."

He seemed to be trying to be generous, so it seemed only fair to reciprocate. "I could be smarter," I admitted. "I'm working on it, with a little help from my friends."

"Good," he said. "Be careful out there, okay?"

"Okay," I said, meekly.

CHAPTER NINE

As I'd anticipated, Mum and Dad weren't nearly as understanding.

"What were you thinking?" Dad moaned, after watching half a dozen different versions of the clip, taken from various angles and distances, none of which had a soundtrack sufficiently blurred to obscure what I was saying.

"Well, as you can clearly see and hear, I wasn't, really," I admitted. "I know that I should have anticipated the possibility, and had a speech prepared, but I hadn't and I didn't. My bad—that's American for *mea culpa*."

"You just can't help it, can you?" he replied, despairingly.

"No," I said. "It used to be considered charming while I was alive—or, at worst, interestingly eccentric. It's amazing what a difference dying can make. Who knew?"

"I don't doubt that there'll be some people watching it who have every sympathy with you," he said, although he plainly did doubt it, "but imagine what effect it will have on the Afro-Anglican community…and any other people with religious sensibilities."

"The jihadists will love it," I said. "After all, I was taking the piss out of infidels. And the Catholics will love it, because I was taking the piss out of Protestants. And the Anglo-Anglicans will love it, because I was taking the piss out the jumped up sods who are trying to steal their Church from under their feet. The only people who will actually hate it are the liberals—and quite frankly, being hated by liberals is a bit like being whipped by a woolly sock full of cotton wool. It's not that bad, Dad."

"We've already had black spots through the post, you know—we didn't want to tell you because we didn't want to upset you."

"Everybody gets black spots, Dad—it's an epidemic. At the Center, we get stones through the window. It's like everything else in life—you just have to hope that the catastrophe wall unfold slowly. My little rant at a trio of pantomime Churchmen is a very tiny drop in a very big ocean. Here today, gone tomorrow."

"If only," was all he said to that—but I don't think he really meant that he wanted *me* gone tomorrow. Not consciously, at any rate.

"He's just worried about you, Nicky," Mum said. "We all are."

"I know, Mum," I said. "I'll be careful in future—I promise."

"Do you honestly think you can keep that promise?" Kirsten asked.

"Yes I do," I told her. "I'm a different person now. I can keep myself in check, now that I've been sharply reminded of the necessity."

"Give you a hard time at the Center, did they?" she enquired. "Letting the side down and all that?"

"Anything but," I admitted. "Leant over backwards to be nice about it, in fact. Made it all the harder to bear—but the ones who said anything at all made it perfectly clear that it was up to me to figure out whether my act needed cleaning up, and how far to go."

"Even Nurse Pearl?" she said. "Surely *she* was sarcastic?"

"She wasn't there," I admitted. "She'll probably be in tomorrow evening, though. I expect she'll rip into me then, if she's in the mood."

"It's only because she worries about you. You're still her patient, in her eyes."

"Maybe so," I said. "I don't mind. Her heart's in the right place, even if some of her living patients are too paranoid to notice. What do you think, Kirsty? Exactly how stupid was I, on a scale of one to ten?"

"Who am I to judge," she replied, judiciously. "I'm just your little sister, brought up from birth in awe of your intelligence and wit. I wouldn't dare criticize. After all, it's not going to rebound on me, is it?"

"God, I hope not," I said, with the utmost sincerity.

* * * * * * *

As I'd predicted to Kirsten, Pearl did come into the Center the following evening, but she was later than would normally have been expected. By the time she arrived, though, we all knew that she'd been doing a harrowing extra shift. She hadn't phoned anyone to tell us, but we knew anyway. If I'd been worried about the possibility of her commenting on my tantrum while I made my way into the Center past all the inquisitive eyes that followed my progress, any lingering anxiety vanished soon after lunch, when the news began to come through about the pile-up at the A329M terminus.

The workstation bots flagged the incident as soon as it was reported, and the people on the mezzanine fed it down to the main floor in dribs and drabs for the rest of the afternoon. By the time Pearl made her belated arrival, we were all on tenterhooks. Since the emergency services had closed off the scene, we'd only had the parsimonious trickle of official information to go on with regard to its seriousness. We knew that she'd have at least some of the inside information, as well as impressions gained at first hand.

"Yes, it was bad," she confirmed, "in more ways than one."

What we already knew was that the brakes had failed on an articulated lorry approaching the roundabout at the junction of the A329M and the A4. It had ploughed straight across the roundabout after sideswiping a couple of cars on the motorway proper, hitting more vehicles as it cut through the lateral traffic on both sides. At least thirty vehicles had been involved in total, and fatalities had been reported. Pearl filled in some of the as-yet-unreleased details.

"Some school run traffic involved. Seven dead thus far, three of them kids. Only one likely to be zombifiable, although they're attempting at least one more. It could have been worse—all the vehicles were braking except for the artic, and even that wasn't traveling very fast, but it skittled the ones it hit, set them cannoning into others like snooker balls. Rumor's doing the rounds that the artic's brakes were sabotaged, but that's just par for the course—probably nonsense.

"To make things worse, five people died on the wards while we were all busy in A and E. Nothing untoward, really, but a couple might have lasted a few days longer if they'd got immediate attention. Unfortunately, the statistical blip is enough to trigger an automatic enquiry, and you know what committees are like when they start trying to justify their own pointless existence. Some poor sod will probably end up being suspended on suspicion of possible negligence, on account of not being able to be in three places at once using five pairs of hands. Andy won't be coming in tonight or tomorrow, but I had to get off the premises, even though I'm dog tired."

There were commiserations all round, as she must have anticipated, but the solicitude soon began to annoy her and she began to shrug off, the gestures of solidarity—which only made the people offering them try extra hard to make their sympathy clear. When Alice's valiant attempts to be maternal became too much, Pearl began to edge from fractiousness into open hostility. Gradually, her prickliness began to drive people away. It was late anyway, so people were beginning to disappear in twos and threes, mostly heading back to the South Street hostel.

By the time there were only half a dozen of us left in the Center, everyone but me—even Stan—was busy on the workstations, indulging their hobbies or catching up with their retraining programs. Pearl was slumped in her chair, sipping from her third cup of tea, and brooding.

"Jim's at home tonight, I'm afraid," I said, "but if he were here, he'd be telling you not to walk home alone, and he'd be right—it's already getting dark."

"My stalker didn't follow me from the hospital tonight," she said, wearily, "and if he was waiting here for me, he obviously had time to get bored and head back home. Anyway, you're not going to get into my knickers, even if I am a trifle overwrought, so there's no point in you volunteering to see me home."

Slightly nettled by that, I fished around for an alternative topic of conversation. "Will you be writing up the day's excitement in your diary? You'll need to do that sort of thing now you've started writing your autobiography."

"I don't need your help with that, either," she retorted, perhaps predictably.

"I don't suppose you do. Nor do Methuselah and Marjorie, really—they just want to be sure that someone's actually reading their stuff."

She snorted derisively. "Marjorie's not short of readers, even now. If she's getting you to look over her stuff it's just because she fancies you as a toy boy. If you want my advice, go for it. You could do worse. She was only forty-nine when she died, and you two have a lot in common."

"I never got around to joining Greenpeace," I told her, although I knew perfectly well what she meant.

"Well, maybe not as much as all that," she admitted. "After all, you were just collateral damage—she was an actual target."

I looked up at the mezzanine to make certain that Marjorie was fully absorbed at her station before saying: "So it's rumored. Who do you think was behind it?"

"My money's on Big Oil," she replied, without any noticeable sarcasm in her tone. "The Russian Mafia branch, in all probability. She must think so too—that's why she's been so careful."

"She's getting back into the swim," I said. "I haven't seen her recent Greenpeace stuff, but if it's anything like her zombie rights material…."

"I know," she said, cutting me off. "I read it all when it's posted. Even though it's not signed, my bot can sieve it out. I only hope that the Russian mob aren't doing the same."

"You think she might still be in danger? Methuselah hinted at it, but I thought he was just being overanxious."

"Maybe so—but if anyone ever comes through that door waving a Kalashnikov, you'd better make sure that you're not standing next to her...unless, of course, you want to take the bullet for her, on the grounds that you're a more likely candidate for reresurrection than she is. There's no need, if all you're interested in is sex. Just say the word and she'll have her knickers off in no time."

I decided to ignore her ongoing preoccupation with items of underwear. "The day people start coming through the door waving assault rifles," I said, soberly, "they'll probably be after all of us. Not that it's likely to happen any time soon—this is Merry England, not the Wild East."

"Grow up, Nicky," she said. "This is multicultural Reading. If ever there was an urban powder-keg waiting for a spark...but you're right: best not to think about it."

"Anyway, I said, "the ED top the terror charts hereabouts, and we're only fourth or fifth on their hate-list. They've already killed me once, so I'd have to be really unlucky to take a second hit, even if they did send Mum and Dad the black spot while I was in hospital."

"Only one? I've had a dozen."

"Why so many?"

"I work in a hospital. I told you the other day, remember? You have no idea how malicious patients can be, when the fear and the stress get on top of them. You've seen them making the sign of the cross—and we all know how bravely unintimidated you are by that sort of thing—but it's what they get up to behind your back that can really do some damage. Multiply what's happened to you since you woke up on the ward by a hundred, and that's pretty much my average week. Zombie nurses are in demand, as you know...but not from a majority of the living patients, that's for sure. Do you know how many times I've been called an angel of death? Not just in a poetic sense, either—some of my less appreciative patients seem to have actually managed to convince themselves that I bump people off on the sly, in order to make more zombies."

I didn't think it was the right time to tell her about the subject of Marjorie latest posting, so I said: "All the more reason why you shouldn't be walking back to the accommodation-block on your own after dark. I know it's only half a mile, but still…why not ask Marjorie and Alice? They can walk you home and then go back to South Street together, if you're really worried about the possibility that I might make a pass at you."

"*You* don't worry me," she said, in a tone that seemed to have reached an extreme of fatigue. "I've been raped by experts."

That had slipped out unawares; she evidently regretted it the moment she'd said it, for more reasons than one. "Sorry," she said, while I was still lost for words. "I didn't mean to imply…."

"No problem," I replied.

The question I'd left unspoken must have been obvious regardless. "Yes," she added, still confused by her error and not knowing quite how to shut up, let alone what to say. "I suppose it was, if only indirectly." She meant that having been raped was at least related to the reason why she'd killed herself.

"It's okay," I told her. "You don't need to say anything at all. Shall I go away? I can ask Marjorie to come and talk to you, if you like—I think she's finished at the workstation now."

"No," she said, to everything. After a pause to collect herself she said: "Things still all right at home, are they?"

It seemed only polite to give every encouragement to her valiant change of subject. "Fine," I said. "I can't get through to my girl-friend yet, but I guess she needs time to get used to the new situation. Mum and Dad are a bit edgy round me, but that's only to be expected, and Dad's begun to displace a little of his unease into uncomfortable discussions. Kirsty's a brick, though—seems to have taken it completely in her stride. She takes her principles seriously, although it probably helps that she thought that I was plenty weird enough while I was alive. Can't imagine why—the age-gap between us should have encouraged hero-worship rather than intersibling animosity."

"I was an only child," was Pearl's only comment on that.

"I'm lucky, I know," I continued, rabbiting on just for the sake of filling the awkward silence, and feeling that I was—for once—on safe ground. "I know exactly how lucky I am. Things really are going as well as can be expected, not just at home but here. I'm settling in. Everyone's been good to me. I have a lot to be thankful for—although I haven't *quite* got around to being grateful to England's Defenders, for defending me so successfully."

I knew it wasn't going to raise a smile, but I felt obliged to put on a show of trying.

Mercifully, Marjorie had indeed, finished at the workstation, and she came down from the mezzanine to join us. I was pleased to see her, having despaired of my own ability to give Pearl the support she evidently needed but somehow couldn't accept.

"I thought you ought to know that there's some net-buzz building up, Pearl," the older woman said, "about the accident and the hospital."

"There's always net-buzz," Pearl said, tiredly.

"Did you know that the driver of the vehicle that caused the crash was a zombie?"

"No," said Pearl, sitting up a little straighter. "He wasn't brought into the Berks—they had to take some of the injured to Battle, and ferried a couple all the way to Abingdon General by helicopter. The paramedics probably separated him from the others on purpose, even though he was just another victim."

Long-distance lorry-driving, I knew, was one of the few jobs to which zombies were often able to go back, largely because it was the kind of job that required minimal interaction with other people. Statistically speaking, it wasn't all *that* surprising that the driver of the runaway artic had been a zombie—but that wouldn't stop the kind of people who crossed their rigid forefingers at poor Pearl from trying to make something of it.

"Surely nobody's claiming that the truck-driver caused the crash deliberately?" I said.

"Not everyone's as careful about what they post as I am,"

Marjorie told me, only a trifle sarcastically.

"But nobody's going to believe that," I said, not entirely confidently. "The rumor that his brakes were sabotaged is surely far more plausible."

"In terms of the calculus of probability, you're right," Marjorie confirmed, "but rationality takes a back seat when netbuzz gets going. There's the mortality blip at the hospital too. Perfectly understandable, of course, in the circumstances, but not entirely coincidental. There are people in the world capable of adding two and two and coming up with ninety-five. And it's just possible—and this *is* coincidental—that I…well, I might not have helped."

"Oh shit!" said Pearl. "What have you done, Marjorie?"

"It's just that…with the aid of hindsight, you might have been right, Nicky, about some of my wording…and the timing maybe isn't ideal. I had no idea, Pearl, honestly. I didn't know about the accident until after I'd posted. The posting's anonymous, of course, but…well, there are people out there who know who I am, and where I am…."

"What have you *done*, Marjorie?" Pearl repeated, icily.

"It's really nothing to worry about," I hastened to put in. "I was being oversensitive yesterday, Marjorie…it's just a hypothetical argument, as you said, relating to an ongoing debate in the public arena. Nobody's going to take the inference that you were actually affirming that the afterliving are morally entitled to go around killing the living…and *nobody*'s going to think it has anything to do with what happened today."

"Advocating *what*?" Pearl put in, showing genuine alarm.

"It was an argument about assisted suicide, really," Marjorie said, defensively. "It's just that Nicky thought…and he might be right…that I might not have made that clear enough."

Pearl swallowed hard, although she hadn't actually taken a gulp of tea. She suppressed the alarm reaction, though, forcing herself to resume a perfect professional tranquility.

"It's a storm in a teacup," I affirmed. "Nothing will come of it."

"You're right," Pearl agreed, with far less certainty than I would have preferred. "Nothing at all."

"Can I walk you home anyway?" I asked. "I won't make a pass—I promise."

"Okay, then," she said, only slightly unexpectedly.

"I'll come with you," Marjorie said. "I promise too."

"Is your promise addressed to me, or to Nicky?" Pearl had sufficient presence of mind to quip—but none of us laughed.

CHAPTER TEN

This is not the place to embark on an elaborate discussion about the unfortunate corollaries of an age of instant communication, when everyone can be a newsgatherer and everyone a commentator. The topic has already been done to death—although I suppose it's also typical of the era that it's continually resurrected. The fact that selectorbots make it easy to string together a series of unconnected data in such a way as to synthesize an apparent pattern and add a suggestion of causality is so familiar that it's surprising that anyone can any longer get suckered in by such frail factoid-combinations.

Unfortunately, the living brain is programmed to look for connections, because the whole basis of rational intelligence is the ability to find them. If only the mental sieve that separates the real connections from the false ones were more efficient, the living brain would be an even greater wonder than it is, and science would long ago have stamped superstition into the ground. Natural selection, alas, is mostly content to produce apparatus sufficient to help people to breed, and the burden of false connection is simply part of our genetic load.

Is it any different for the afterliving? Is the resurrected brain any better at applying the filter that separates out the intellectual wheat from the superstitious chaff? The simple answer, I suppose, is no—but in my opinion, it's not as simple as that. I prefer to say: *not yet*.

The afterliving brain is not a product of natural selection. Nobody is naïve enough to believe that twenty-first-century

Resurrection Men don't discriminate, to a greater extent than the law demands and permits, and that makes the selection even more unnatural than it would otherwise be. Success in breeding is not an issue for the afterliving—not yet, anyhow—so the only things that matter, in determining the intellectual spectrum of the afterliving community, are who gets reborn and how long they afterlive. It's not evident yet that the Mighty Burkers are showing a prejudice in favor of the scientifically-minded, but even if they aren't, it *is* very evident that the unscientifically-minded are prejudiced against *them*. On average, therefore, one would expect the afterliving community—which has to be seen as a community, rather than merely a collection of individuals, because the phenomenon in question is collective as well as individual—to have better filters than the living community.

Nor is that the whole of the matter, because the filters in question aren't fixed; they develop, and they remain capable of further development. If all else were equal, one would expect the afterliving community to develop better filters over time simply because of its members' protracted longevity, but there are other factors in play too. I would contend, strongly, that the experience of afterlife is, in itself, conducive to persona development of that sort. Simply by virtue of being able to stand outside the living community, one gets a clearer view of its follies, and when one is very likely to suffer from the fallout of those follies, even at the trivial levels of being subjected to attempted exorcisms by errant Afro-Anglicans, one is also very likely to have one's awareness of their absurdity sharpened.

In brief, we zombies start off, on average, smarter than the living, and everything we experience is conducive to making us progressively smarter still—and when I say *progressively*, I mean it. Not that I'm implying that the living are no longer making progress, of course—Heaven forbid!—but I am implying, in my own sweet way, that of all the progress that is being currently being made in the world, and is likely to be made in the future, if any of us have a future, a disproportionate amount of it is being and will be made by the afterliving. It's politically incorrect to say so, of course, but what the hell. The truth will out, and the truth is that we're not only already better than you are, and getting further ahead all the time, but that you ought to be as glad of the fact as we are.

After all, if zombies don't save the world from the godawful mess that the living have left it in after a hundred thousand years of sole control, who will?

All we need is time, and the freedom to act.

Will we get it?

Who can tell?

* * * * * * *

By the time I got back home, it was late. Dad and Mum had already gone to bed, but Kirsten was still up, ostensibly watching TV.

"I was worried about you," she said. "I thought something might have happened."

"Because of the accident on the A329M?"

"No, you idiot—because of your little tirade yesterday morning. Even Christians can get violent, and it's bound to have put you on the ED radar."

"It's okay," I told her. "Marjorie and I walked Pearl back to the hospital, and then I walked Marjorie back to the hostel. Then I came home. We didn't have any trouble, although I did notice a number of twitching curtains."

"Okay—you could have rung, though."

"Sorry."

"Well, I suppose it could have been worse—Marjorie might have invited you in for coffee."

"What she actually said," I informed her, "was: 'I was going to invite you in for coffee, but I was afraid you might deliberately misunderstand me and say that you had to get off home, so how you would like to come upstairs and do as many filthy things as you can think of to me, until I have an orgasm'."

The look of pure horror on my little sister's face was amusing for the first twenty seconds or so, but when it didn't disappear it became a trifle worrying.

"Only joking," I told her. "She did invite me in for coffee, but I said I had to get off home. I have no idea whether I was misunderstanding her or not."

The look of horror disappeared, but all Kirsten could think of to say thereafter was: "She's forty-nine."

"No she isn't," I retorted. "If you count from her birthday, she's fifty-two, and if you count from her rebirthday, she's three. Mind you, if you count from my rebirthday I'm only a few weeks old, so that would make her something of a cradle-snatcher, if I wasn't misunderstanding."

"You're impossible," she said.

"I know," I agreed, "but I don't care."

"And you're not funny."

"So I'm finding out. It's the hardest lesson of all."

She had recovered somewhat—enough to say: "Well, if there's a next time, give us a ring to let us know that you're okay, and then you can accept any invitations you get, whoever they're from."

"I can only love Marjorie like a sister," I said. "I've already got a girl-friend."

Her recovery had proceeded far enough to permit a smidgen of malice. "I remember her," Kirsten said. "Nice girl. What was her name again?"

"And Marjorie's dangerous to know as well as mad and bad," I told her. "The Russian mob are after her, Kalashnikovs waving—so don't tell anyone you know where she is, okay?" With that, I went to bed, feeling that I'd won the exchange at least five-two.

The next day, I knew as soon as I got up in the morning that the shit had hit the fan. Dad was still a traditionalist, if not to the extent of buying a newspaper made from processed wood-pulp, at least to the extent of having his laptop open on the breakfast table so that he could bring himself up to date with the weather forecast, the cricket scores and the closing prices on the world's ailing stock markets. Naturally, he had bots set to bring anything newsworthy that happened within a five-mile radius to his attention.

"Do you know a woman named Marjorie Claridge?" he asked me, before I'd even taken the top of my boiled egg—causing Kirsten to look up sharply from hers.

The first thing that occurred to me was that Dad might somehow have overheard what I'd said to Kirsten the night before, so I blushed scarlet, but I collected myself almost immediately. "Yes," I said. "She comes to the Center every day. Why?"

"And what was the name of that nurse at the hospital? The one your mother thought was *nice*?"

That got Mum's lingering attention. She was very sensitive to implicit insults, even at seven-thirty in the morning.

"She *is* nice," I said, more for Mum's benefit than Pearl's. "Her name's Pearl Barleigh."

"I bet is it," Dad sneered, obviously unconvinced by the unwisdom or humorlessness of poor Pearl's parents, even though it would surely have been unwiser still to adopt such a name as a pseudonym. "It says here that she's under investigation."

I knew that I wasn't capable any longer of going pale, even when I'd just blushed scarlet, so I couldn't be sure that anyone was able to judge my reaction, but I felt as if a cruel hand was squeezing my heart. "For what?" I said, although I wasn't in any doubt.

"For possible involvement in the death of three patients at the Royal Berks yesterday—and a dozen more over the last couple of months."

"It's garbage," I said, instantly. "It's absolutely untrue."

I could see immediately that it wasn't going to wash—not with Mum and Dad, at any rate. It was one thing to take me back into their loving home, and to continue to treat me as their beloved son in spite of everything, but that was as far as their generosity went; my fate had put their attitudes to the afterliving under greater stress.

"You don't understand," I said—although it was hardly the most diplomatic opening. "Fear alones generates a trickle of accusations, and the hospital admin knows perfectly well that they're rubbish—but that doesn't stop them building up and building up, until it only takes one last straw to shatter the camel's back. But the admin still know it's rubbish—they might be forced to set up an investigative committee, but the committee will exonerate her, and issue a press release to say that there was absolutely no truth in the allegations."

I knew even as I said it that, though, that it might take more than an eventual official clearance to save Pearl's precarious career, no matter how much demand there was for zombie nurses at present, or how much valiant propaganda the BBC pumped out on *Resurrection Ward*.

"But she does know this Marjorie Claridge, doesn't she?" Dad queried, as if that were the trump card on his side of the argument...given that there did seem to be an argument, and that he did seem to have taken a side.

"So do I, Dad—what's that supposed to prove?"

Dad could go pale, and did, as a new thought occurred to him. "You're not in on it too, are you?" he said. "You've only been a bloody zombie for a fortnight!"

"In on what?" I demanded. Because I was sitting opposite, I couldn't see the screen of the laptop, although Mum and Kirsten were both leaning sideways to peek.

"It says that the police have been called in to investigate allegations of a conspiracy regarding yesterday's crash on the roundabout at the entrance to the Industrial Park," Kirsten put in, helpfully. "It doesn't say who made the allegations, which presumably means that it was some nutter calling the shop-your-neighbor helpline."

"But neither Pearl not Marjorie knew the driver," I said, helplessly.

Dad could be a bit of an idiot sometimes, but he was no fool. "You mean that you've already *talked to them* about this?" he said. "You *knew* about it? Oh, Nicky—how could you be so *stupid?*"

"How can there be a conspiracy if there's no fucking connection?" I replied, not realizing until the words were out that I'd shouted them, and that I was standing up, pink with outrage.

"Sit down and finish your boiled egg, Nicky," was Mum's contribution to the discussion—perhaps the only truly sensible one that could have been made at that point.

Kirsten had reached out to tap the keys on Dad's machine. "It seems," she said, "that the driver of the artic—who walked away with a few bruises, by the way—was on a retraining program with one of Marjorie's *known associates*, who didn't get a job at the end of it. Stanley Blake?"

I sat down, although I didn't pick up my egg-spoon. "We're all on retraining programs, all the bloody time," I told her. "If one in a hundred leads to a job, it's a near-miracle. For the final exam, I suppose, Stan presumably had to turn up to sit in an actual vehicle, but I'll lay odds that he did ninety per cent of it sitting on the mezzanine in the Center, with one of the workstations running simulation programs. I doubt that he ever even met the guy. He's being...." I stopped then, not sure if even Kirsten would be able to believe me if I carried on.

"So you know *him* too?" Dad said. "Jesus, Nicky, you're going to be implicated in this. Even if you're not part of the conspiracy, you're going to be dragged in. Thank God you've only been going to the Center for a fortnight. You can't go back. You have to contact the police, and tell them what you know."

This time, I was careful not to stand up or shout. I even picked up my egg-spoon, in order to demonstrate my perfect composure.

"There is no conspiracy, Dad," I said. "At least, not at the Center. If there is a conspiracy, we're its victims, not its perpetrators. Pearl isn't an angel of death and she isn't being manipulated by evil zombie rights campaigners. Yesterday's accident was an accident, unless some malicious bastard—living bastard—sabotaged the driver's brakes because he doesn't approve of the afterliving being allowed to drive heavy goods vehicles while there are living men on the dole. Either way, the only possible conspiracy here is the one that's trying to stitch up Marjorie, Pearl and Stan."

"And who would want to do that?" Dad asked, skeptically.

I didn't dare tell him. It would have sounded way too paranoid, even to me. I excavated a spoonful of egg instead.

"The ED sent us a black spot before Nicky had even recovered consciousness," Kirsten chipped in. "And Marjorie Claridge had enough enemies while she was alive to get her killed. If she's still involved in green politics as well as zombie rights, they're probably still her enemies, and they'd probably jump at any opportunity to sling mud at her—or put a bullet in her." She'd obviously taken due note of what I'd said the night before.

"Ridiculous," was Dad's judgment. He was the sort of person who would never believe that the Russian Mafia was now the clandestine branch of Big Oil's public relations department. I was still finding it difficult to swallow myself—almost as difficult as Mum's boiled egg, although it had still had a lovely liquid yolk, and certainly wouldn't have caused any diplomatic difficulties to a visiting curate.

"Your Dad's right, though," Mum put in. "You can't go to the Center today, Nicky. It's a good job you can do your training program on your own computer."

"I don't want to miss rockmobility," I said, frostily. "The afterliving have to keep fit—we have to look after ourselves."

"That's not the point, and you know it," Dad told me, sternly. "You shouldn't go. You need to stay out of this, if you possibly can. If there's nothing to it, it'll blow over. If not…well, either way, the sensible thing to do is stay home until it's sorted." He wasn't trying to forbid me, though, because he knew he no longer had that authority—not because I was twenty-seven years old, but because I was dead. That was a shame, in a way, because it meant I had to match reason with reason…and that was difficult, because there as a sense which he was right. The sensible thing to do *was* to stay out of it, until it was sorted.

"I'm going to the Center," I said, flatly. "Everybody will."

"But you don't have to," Mum protested.

"Of course he does," Kirsten put in. I met her eyes, and gave her a grateful nod.

Dad was all reason now, though. "I can see why you might think that," he said, "if you're convinced that there really isn't a conspiracy, and that these people really are your friends—but how much do you know about them, really? How do you know what that nurse might be doing? Have you read what this Claridge woman writes? If the excerpt they've quoted here is correct…."

"It's probably taken out of context, Dad," I said, wanting to short-circuit the possibility of his reading it aloud. "And yes—I have read what she writes. I'm the one who corrects her punctuation. I'm in this up to my neck."

"You didn't think to suggest that she might tone it down a bit?" Dad said, raising a quizzical eyebrow.

"No," I lied. "The afterliving are entitled to philosophize just like everyone else, and the right to publish their conclusions, anonymously or otherwise."

"And you're a zombie now," he said, following through. "After two lousy weeks, you're a zombie, and nothing else. All your loyalties have been recalculated, all your lines redrawn."

"That's not fair, Dad," Kirsten said—but he already knew that. The unfairness was deliberate. He was making a point. Everybody has the right to philosophize, and to make their conclusions known.

"If you were the ones under threat," I said, including all three of them in the pronoun, "no matter where the threat was coming from, I wouldn't step out of the door. You're not. Pearl is."

"I thought you were still in love with Helena?" Mum queried.

"I am," I told her. "There's nothing between me and Pearl—or between me and Marjorie, for that matter. We all made that perfectly clear before Marjorie and I walked Pearl back to the accommodation block last night. I don't doubt that we were seen, even though Pearl's living stalker had taken the night off. As I said, I'm in it up to my neck. The CCTV pictures have probably been pinned up on an incident-board by now. But there's nothing to it except malicious rumor and paranoia, and the police must know that. The investigation is just a matter of following obligatory procedure. If they try to contact me here, tell them where I am."

I stood up again.

"You haven't finished your breakfast," Mum said—but it was a token protest, and not entirely accurate. I'd just about cleaned out the egg-shell, and I picked up the last piece of toast to take with me.

I was glad to get out of the house, though—at least until I started walking along the street. Even if it hadn't been for the new scandal, I'd already done enough to make that half-mile walk an exhibition-piece. Even before the incident with the exorcist, I'd been conscious of the fact that people were looking at me as I passed by, but until I'd lost my rag I'd been able to tell myself that it was just my own paranoia, and that the feeling would wear off. That option wasn't open any more, and the knowledge that everyone in the neighborhood had read the same combination of real and imaginary "news" as Dad multiplied my anxiety by a factor of ten.

Most people, though, still looked away rather than meet my eye, even if the immediate neighbors no longer wanted to say hello. Only a minority stared—and only a small minority bothered to aim their phones at me as I walked past. One or two of them did follow me, filming all the while, but that was only because they thought that there was a remote possibility that something might happen, not because they were convinced that something would.

"This is a storm in a teacup," I told himself, subvocalizing the words. "The background is that zombies have already become so familiar that nobody really gives them a second glance any more, especially in a town like Reading, which is as conspicuously multicultural as any town in England, except Slough, Leicester and Bradford."

It was no good. I didn't even bother chiding myself for

my lack of trust. I just made every possible effort to hold my ominous consciousness in check, while I took the journey to the Center one step at a time.

Nobody even shouted at me, let alone spat or shot at me. Whatever the people watching me were thinking—and the words "smoke," "without" and "fire" inevitably came to mind—they kept it to themselves. The ones who were fortunate enough to have jobs had to get to work, and even the ones who didn't had places to go, just as I had. Even the ones who followed me hastened away when I reached the Center.

I couldn't help looking up at the sandstone lintel, which still retained its memory of William Booth's heroic institution, even though the ever-dwindling organization he'd founded had abandoned it to the care of the Borough Council at least forty years before.

Could General Booth ever have imagined, I wondered, that some tiny fraction of his legacy would one day become a refuge for the kindred of Lazarus? If so, would he too have considered us demons, or would his pragmatic non-conformism have taken a Christian view even of the risen dead?

Either way, there seemed to be a measure of irony in my crossing the threshold.

CHAPTER ELEVEN

Alcohol has exactly the same effect on an afterliving body as it does on a living one. That's not at all surprising, given that the physiology of afterlife is so similar to the physiology of life. What is surprising is, though, that is that zombies, by and large, don't get drunk. They can and they could, but they don't. Even zombies who were alcoholics in life tend to become very moderate drinkers once they've been resurrected. Rumor has it that similar generalizations apply to heavy smokers and heroin addicts, although the sample sizes are currently too small to be statistically significant.

The consensus seems to be that the difference is a matter of personality. The afterliving, it's generally agreed, are much less prone to have addictive personalities of any sort than the living. Those who drink find it a lot easier to stop drinking before the effects of alcohol begin to impair their judgment, and the same applies to other pleasant-but-potentially-harmful experiences. Zombies who were clinically obese in life—again, not a vast sample, but not negligible either—start off their afterlives still obese, but almost all of them lose weight progressively, until they reach the supposedly normal height-to-weight ratio. Like those who carry the legacy of aging through into their afterlives, they never recover the vigor typical of young athletes, but they don't usually retain the full extent of the burdens they bore in life.

Scientifically-minded commentators, not unnaturally, try to subsume the typical patterns of alcohol use and abuse in afterlife to the more general debate about the appetites of the afterliving. Just as certain other kinds of cravings are weakened, the argument goes, the craving for alcohol is weakened too. With respect to ex-addicts, the hypothesis often expands to embrace the case that all the changes of appetite associated with afterlife derive from alterations in the endogenous morphine and other neurotransmitter-damping systems: in brief, the allegation is that zombies don't suffer from withdrawal symptoms, at least to the same extent as the living. That's a hypothesis to which I'm not unsympathetic, although I'm withholding my final judgement until Andy Hazelhurst and his peers have collected more hard evidence.

The most popular theory among the unscientifically-minded—which inevitably owes its popularity to its supposed aesthetic propriety rather that to any scientific proof—is that death is an essentially sobering and salutary experience: that once a person has died, the individual in question find it difficult to be reckless with the stuff of afterlife. That one is, of course, poppycock.

For one thing—and one's enough to kill the hypothesis—nobody actually remembers dying. Even the afterliving who undergo radical transformations of personality because of the extensive repair-work required by their brains—which presumably includes most of the heavy drinkers and other chronic self-abusers—don't wake up with any sense of no longer being alive, or of having had their lives suspended. It's only the living who sometimes wake up from surgical interventions to report out-of-body experiences and visions of being drawn toward some kind of uncanny light.

Personally, I'm convinced that, whatever the physiological detail might be, afterlife sobriety really is intrinsic to the zombie condition. What's more, I'm inclined, once again, to come right out and say that if that makes us, on average, better people than the living, then that's just the way it is. It's not only our privilege but our responsibility.

What I mean by that is that it's up to us to set an example

to our weaker brethren—and if we have to take over the world to do it, then we should. It's our moral entitlement, and our moral duty. We have to do it peacefully, though, while strictly observing the principle of informed consent—not just because that's the diplomatic way to proceed, but because that's the kind of sober, scientifically-minded people we are.

Or, at least, the kind of people we ought to aspire to be.

* * * * * * *

The hall was already crowded when I went in, and already noisy.

Pearl was complaining bitterly that her suspension from work had effectively painted a target on her back, and that the hospital accommodation block was no longer a safe place or her to be. She seemed more angry than scared, but she was probably just displacing her fear into her anger.

Marjorie was apologizing to all and sundry for having retained all the reckless habits she'd acquired during long service with Greenpeace. She seemed genuinely sorry, although I doubt that anyone believed that regret was going to make her change her behaviour.

Stan was telling off Jim Peel yet again, instructing him in a typically forceful manner as to the necessity of meekness and careful diplomacy in all circumstances. He might have been more convincing if he hadn't been as tense as a coiled spring himself. The contrast between his invariable black T-shirt and his pale but artificially-colored arms put me in mind of a collie with an ornamental collar-and-tag.

Andy Hazelhurst, who had obviously found the time to come along after all, in spite of Pearl's assurance that he wouldn't be able to, was assuring Methuselah that he would do everything humanly possible to lay the absurd turbulence to rest, in his capacity as a rising star of the Royal Berks Burkers.

The local police officer—who was actually a volunteer "community support officer"—was assuring everyone that a patrol car would make regular passes to ensure that no ugly crowds would be allowed to build up on our doorstep, and that any call for help emanating from the Center would be given top priority…but that CID would be sending a team round as soon as they had completed the preliminary briefing, in order to interview every last one of us.

I headed for Pearl, who seemed to be the person most in need of visible support. "You're an idiot, Nicky," was her expectable greeting. "*You* could have stayed at home. You've only been a zombie for a fortnight, damn it."

"Once a zombie, always a zombie," I told her. "Loyalties recalculated, lines redrawn."

"It'll all blow over," she assured me.

"Storm in a teacup," I replied.

Marjorie tried to buttonhole me then, presumably in order to personalize the latest round of her apologies, but Stan Blake grabbed me first, and drew me to one side.

"Look, Son," he said, "I think I'm going to need your help tonight. You're the youngest one here, and, apart from me, the fittest—Jim included. Tempers are going to flare, inside and out, especially when the paparazzi get out of bed. It's not going to be easy to keep a lid on, but we just have to get through today. Tomorrow, it will all be a lot easier, and by the beginning of next week, it'll all be forgotten, but today…can I rely on you to help me if anything kicks off?"

"I'll do what I can," I promised. "Are you going ahead with rockmobility?"

"Absolutely, if CID give us time. The discipline of planned movement is essential in circumstances like these. There's nothing better to create a mood of solidarity."

"Maybe not," I conceded, "but just for once, if you can bear to do it, it might be a good idea to leave *Highway to Hell* and *Street-Fighting Man* out of the repertoire. Given that you have to stick to the classics, because your technics are way out of date, try *Two Tribes* and *Jumping Jack Flash* instead."

He slapped me on the back. "Good lad," he said. "I knew

your heart was in the right place." I think he was complimenting my feigned taste in prehistoric music.

Marjorie managed to capture me then. "I'm sorry, Nicky," she said. "They'll have pictures of the three of us walking back to the Berks, and pictures of you walking me back home afterwards. If anyone takes the wrong implication…."

"They'll know that we parted company on the doorstep of the hostel," I said. "I think your reputation for chastity is safe—I didn't even give you a goodnight kiss."

She didn't laugh, although she nodded to acknowledge the joke. "I should be so lucky," she said. "But just in case anyone should come through that door today waving a Kalashnikov, make sure you hit the ground fast—and stay down, whatever happens."

"It's not going to happen," I assured her. "Even if we only get a handful of authentic paparazzi camping on our doorstep, there'll be dozens of locals with phones at the ready. No self-respecting hit-man would dream of exposing himself to so many avid cameras. You're safer today than you were yesterday."

"Look after yourself," she said. "I mean it."

"I know you do," I assured her. "I've only been a newreborn for a fortnight, but I'm beginning to realize what a hot property this body is. You can see how hard it is for Pearl to suppress her raging lust, and I'm grateful to you for making the effort yourself."

She punched me on the shoulder then, but she still didn't laugh. I think she was probably grateful for the fact that zombies can't cry.

The paparazzi started arriving at nine o'clock; ours wasn't the kind of scandal that could get them out of bed at the crack of dawn after a hard night's celebrity-stalking. Andy Hazelhurst had already made himself scarce. By the time the CID team arrived at ten-thirty, causing rockmobility to be suspended while Stan and I were still going strong, there were a dozen suspicious characters lurking in the vicinity with their fancy digital cameras at the ready, but they were sticking to the rules and not giving anyone any hassle—least of all the CID officers.

The police had rules of their own to observe; while the CID were inside the Center they posted a uniformed officer on the door—a real officer, not a Mickey Mouse volunteer—to make absolutely certain that nothing unpleasant would happen while they were there to witness it. Their jobs were complicated enough already. The community support officer set off to patrol the community supportively, following a script that required her presence to be polite and unobtrusive.

The plain-clothed policemen were exceedingly polite when they broke up the rockmobility session—while Stan, teeth-gritted, was listening to his obsolete apparatus blast out *Walking on Sunshine*—and they were relentlessly efficient in organizing timetables for the individual interviews, which were to be conducted by three officers strategically placed in different corners of the hall.

I was one of the first in line, although I had no clue as to the logic of the selective procedure.

"Don't rush it, Mate," Stan whispered in my ear, when was called forward. "The longer they're here, the better." I took proud note of the fact that I had been promoted from "Son" to "Mate," after a mere fortnight of casual acquaintance. I put it down to my proven rockmobility endurance.

My interviewer was a D.C. Niles: a young man only a year or two younger than me, with ambition practically oozing out of his pores. I didn't need to worry about spinning it out; he was obviously determined to give me an exceedingly thorough grilling, if only for form's sake.

I explained that, despite the short length of our acquaintance, I felt that I knew Pearl and Marjorie very well, and had every confidence in their probity, that we had only been in one another's company the previous evening because we were trying to help one another out, and that the very idea of afterliving individuals formulating conspiracies in order to increase the rate of their recruitment for the living was beyond ludicrous. I was certain that he believed me, and that he was probably grateful to have the case so eloquently made for the benefit of his tape.

The interviews with Pearl, Marjorie and Stan, which were held simultaneously, took a lot longer; indeed, they dragged on for hours, although I don't think that the dragging was due to any heroic efforts on their part.

"This is daft," Jim Peel muttered, as the rest of us huddled in the fourth corner of the room drinking our umpteenth coffee of the day. "They're not really questioning them about whatever stupid story they got from their anonymous tipster—they're gathering intelligence on the community. The only reason you got away so quickly is that you've only been here a fortnight. They won't be able to pin this on us, obviously, but that won't deter them from keeping a close eye on us, waiting for us to slip up."

"It'll be a long wait, then, won't it?" I said. "Time is on our side. The only way is up."

"When you've been dead as long as I have, Nicky," he told me, sourly, "you won't be so bloody optimistic. The more progress we make, the more resentment will build up against us. If we dodge the explosion this time, it'll only make it more violent when it finally comes."

"If you were prepared to switch rules," I suggested, "we'd be able to put together a soccer team considerably sooner than a rugby union side—even if we have to start off playing five-a-side. If we had an entire team of our own, we might find it easier to get games."

He didn't tell me off for changing the subject. "Built for the scrum, me," he said, mournfully. "Not exactly nimble, even if I have dropped a couple of stone since Stan started me dancing."

"You can be our central defender, then," I told him. "Stan will play, if we ask him nicely, so we only need two more. Mike can probably be drafted, at least as a stopgap, and the season doesn't start for another two months, so...."

"They won't let us into the league, you know."

"I'm not so sure," I told him. "They might be glad to sign us up. Nobody's going to object to playing against us, unless and until we start winning. We just have to take it easy until we've been fully accepted, and then we can really show them what we're made of."

He managed a wry smile at that. "All we really need," he said, "is for the Chelsea team bus to crash on the M4 on the way back from a pre-season friendly—except, of course, that you and I wouldn't stand a chance of getting a game once we had some real players in the ranks."

"The problem with jokes like that," I said, sadly, "is that not only are they not funny, which is forgivable, but that anyone overhearing you, especially today, might get the wrong idea—which isn't."

"I know," he said, mournfully. "It's a bugger, isn't it. Can't remember the last time I had a good laugh." He seemed to be feeling better than he had been when the conversation started, though.

When Pearl had finally been given leave to go, we hastened to rally round. Jim had a cup of coffee ready and waiting for her—which was a pity, because she only drank tea.

"I don't know whether to be glad or disappointed that they haven't arrested me," she said. "I can't help suspecting that I might be safer in custody, until the Hospital Trust can get through its round of committee meetings and issue a press release declaring me utterly blameless. Even then...."

"We've ordered in a stack of pizzas from Domino's," Jim told her. "You do eat pizzas, don't you?" He was still worried about the coffee blunder, which he felt reflected badly on him, given the length of time he'd supposedly known Pearl. I gathered that she'd been keeping him at more than arm's length.

"We were just discussing applying to the local five-a-side league to enter a team," I told her. "By the time the season starts for real, we'll probably be in a position to field a decent five, with a couple of subs on hand."

"I don't play football," she said, shortly, but added: "I do eat pizza, though."

We ate the pizzas while watching the CID team packing up

their stuff, preparing to leave. Purely by coincidence—or so I assumed—it was just coming up to five o'clock: the end of the standard working day. Stan suggested finishing off the rockmobility session that had been interrupted, but he was voted down unanimously.

Marjorie went straight to her workstation as soon as she finished her slice of pizza, and started hammering away on the keyboard. Something told me that she wasn't catching up on her latest retraining course. I hoped that she'd let me see what she wrote before posting it, and would take more notice of any suggestions I made than she had the last time. She wasn't the only one busy in that way; even if I'd had the inclination to catch up with my own course-in-progress, I'd have had difficulty getting on to a machine. I didn't doubt that the newscasters would be monitoring our traffic attentively, and could only hope that the eager typists would be extra careful with the wording of whatever they were pouring into cyberspace. If they were picking up any net-buzz, it wasn't important enough for them to pass it on.

When the remains of the pizzas had been tidied away and more tea and coffee drunk, there seemed to be nothing to do, for those of us not on the machines, but wait, not knowing what it was that we were waiting for.

"Are you intending to stay here all night?" Marjorie asked me.

"Yes," I said. "Are you?"

"Damn right. Not exactly going to be comfortable, though, is it? I count twenty-nine of us. There are two bunks in the storeroom, but apart from that there are only the armchairs, and only eight of those. We'll have to sleep in shifts."

"I wasn't really expecting to sleep," I said. "Stan's right, of course—tonight is crucial. If we get through it unscathed, the heat will leak out of the situation like helium from a balloon. Tomorrow night, most of us will probably be able go home without risk. At least it's midsummer. It won't get dark until half past nine, and it won't get cold at all."

"Most riots happen in high summer," she informed me. "Rain and frost cool drunken ardor—but at this time of year, too many of the living start drinking early, finish late and still feel full of beans in the belated twilight."

"It's okay," I assured her, pointing out of the window—whose external bars, I must confess, I was glad to contemplate for once. "No drunken mob would be able to force their way through the professional paparazzi and the amateur video cowboys—and even if most of those idiots leaning on the lamp-posts are mere gawkers, they aren't getting drunk while they're there, are they?"

"They don't look very dangerous," she conceded, "But the mere fact that anyone's there at all suggests that they expect something to kick off. Is that Pearl's stalker over there on the right, under the tree?"

"I think so," I said. "Well, at least we can be sure that he's harmless, even if he does seem to have kitted himself out in camouflage gear from the local Army & Navy Stores. I reckon they whole lot are a bunch of sheep, most of whom couldn't even be bothered to put on their wolf's clothing."

"You really are walking on sunshine today, aren't you?" she observed.

"Sure," I said. "I got help from one of the on-line agony aunts. Always maintain an optimistic attitude, and it will make you irresistible to women. If there's one thing lonely women hate worse than the absence of a gee-ess-oh-aitch, it's a glass-half-empty kind of guy."

"Better be careful, Nicky," she said. "You don't want to make yourself too irresistible. A pretty boy like you could get into trouble that way."

"Promises, promises," I said—and finally won a thin smile.

By nine o'clock, the crowd still hadn't shown the slightest sign of getting ugly. The authentic paparazzi were looking at their watches, wondering if it might be time to call it a day or go night-club haunting, but they didn't dare make a move just in case one of the opposition ended up getting something they'd missed. Some of the idlers who'd just stopped by to see what was happening did move on, but they were always replaced. The crowd was still growing, albeit gradually.

"Maybe we ought to take Stan's blaster out into the street," Marjorie suggested, "and do a rockmobility session there. It's give them something to watch—and maybe they'd all join in, like one big happy family." She was obviously making an effort not to be a glass-half-empty kind of gal, perhaps in the hope of impressing me.

"Nah," said Stan. "The more it resembles a silent vigil, the better I like it. Don't want to whip up any excitement."

"They're waiting for dusk," Jim said, obviously not having read any good advice columns lately. "Just waiting for darkness to fall."

"If I went back home," Pearl put in, "they'd probably let the rest of you alone." Nobody even dignified that with an answer.

Jim was right, though as it turned out. "They" really were waiting for dusk.

We didn't even know who "they" were until they put in their appearance, but as soon as they did, we were left in no doubt.

We heard them before we actually saw them, and what we heard was unmistakable: the sound of marching boots.

They were probably Doc Martens rather than genuine army boots, although the latter were feely available at the local Army & Navy, but it didn't really matter, as long as they made the right noise.

Tramp, tramp, tramp, they went, as the boots in Kipling's poem should have done, although he had made the tag line *boots, boots, boots*—which is, when you think about it, inappropriate, because "boots" is not an onomatopoeic word.

My heart sank as soon as I heard the tramping, but I joined the others at the window anyway, to see exactly what kind of monstrosity it was that was heading our way.

CHAPTER TWELVE

If this story is ever to be submitted to an arbiter in the hope that it might one day see electronic print through commercial channels, I expect that the first thing a prospective editor will recommend is that I take out almost all of the introductory sections to the chapters, especially this one.

"Nobody's interested in what you think," he or she will undoubtedly tell me, "especially if all you're thinking about is trying to find explanations for things nobody cares about. Nobody's interested in explanations. When they're reading a story, whether it's true or not, all people are interested in is *what happens next*. Telling them what you think, and trying to explain things, just gets in the way. What you need, if you're ever going to interest people in what you're writing, is much less thinking, no explanations at all, and lots more things *happening*. You have to drum it into your head until it becomes second nature: never mind the thinking, *just get on with the story*.

To which my reflexive reply, ironically enough, might be reckoned unprintable by people of delicate sensibility, even in electronic ink. Rather than merely lose my rag, however, I shall try to explain.

The fundamental point is that this is my autobiography—or a slice of it, at any rate—and it wouldn't be authentic if it didn't reflect the real me. It has to be true, not merely to the facts of what happened, but to my point of view.

The simple fact is that I really do spend much of my time thinking, and much of my thinking time hunting for explanations. I can't claim that I always find them, let alone that I always find the right ones, but the story of my life was, in essence, the story of my idle intellectual questing, and the story of my afterlife has been a straightforward extrapolation of the quests in question, minus the idleness. The things that happen, on the rare occasions when things do, are merely décor: background, not foreground.

Maybe that makes me unusual, even among the present-day afterliving, but that doesn't matter. Even if it doesn't exist right now, if I'm right, my ideal audience will eventually materialize. Not that I'm only writing this for my fellow zombies, mind. I think the living can get just as much out of it as the risen dead, if only they're prepared to make the effort.

I'm sorry about the effort, but not *that* sorry. However true it might be that people who read stories are only interested in what happens next, they oughtn't to be. When you think about it, what happens next is only the particular unlikely event that chances to fall out of the chaos of unrealized possibility, and if you hadn't noticed, writers cheat. Million-to-one shots are meat and drink to them. Even so, the implication remains that something else could easily have happened instead, and if time could turned back so that the situation were replayed, it probably would have done. What happens next is, therefore, essentially trivial—but whatever happens, the same questions always remain, the same issues are at stake, the same processes stand in need of explanation. Whatever happens, or doesn't, it all needs thinking about. If you don't do it, who will? Me, obviously—but is that really enough, whether from my viewpoint or yours?

I *am* prepared to apologize for interrupting the story, not just now but continually, but I would like you to think about why I'm doing it. Is it just because I'm a zombie, do you suppose? Is it just because I'm possessed of zombie sobriety, as gloriously free from what-happened-next addition as I am from all other unhealthily gluttonous appetites?

Well, perhaps. Who am I to judge?

It really doesn't matter, though, at the end of the day, exactly what I am. What matters is what I aspire to be, and whether it's something worthy of aspiration. And what matters when the story is over and done with, however it turns out, is what it makes you think about, and what explanations it invites you to look for. Or, to put it another way, what assistance it gives you, however trivial, to make up *your* mind about what *you* should aspire to be.

Is that pompous, or what?

Stories are only trash, after all.

But it doesn't really matter what you or your inner editor might think—not to me. It's not as if I'm alive. I'm dead, if not yet gone—and whatever people might think of them, zombies don't cry.

* * * * * * *

"It's the fucking ED," said Stan, with a theatrical groan. "Why, oh, why, couldn't it have been a column of Afro-Anglican exorcists, or even a pack of wailing jihadists? At least they rant before they get violent, and usually content themselves with just the ranting. The ED haven't got the brains for ranting, unfortunately."

It occurred to me then that I hadn't seen a single religious nut all day—which would have been odd, if I'd thought about it… except that this was the age of the internet, and crazy people always kept tabs on one another as well as on the sane. We hadn't known that England's Defenders had planned some sort of operation, but the Afro-Anglicans probably had, if only because England's Defenders would have sent them a text warning them to stay clear or get stomped.

Within five seconds, Stan had locked the doors. It would have been nice if he'd hauled a massive beam of wood out of his store-room, and if there had been slots riveted to the wall on either side of the door into which the beam might be slotted, but the Salvation Army had never had the need for that kind of provision and Reading Borough Council had certainly not been about to repair the omission.

The reason that a protective beam of that sort would have been useful is that the ED's marching stormtroopers were being assisted to keep in step, in spite of never having put in any real drill practice, by the fact that they were carrying a huge battering-ram.

At a guess, it had actually started out its working life as a telegraph pole—it was certainly impressively long as well as worryingly stout—but no one in the Hall could doubt for an instant what the ED intended to do with it. They were not only going to break in, but to make a show out of breaking in, for the benefit of the waiting cameras.

I made a rapid count of our blessings, and came up with a total of four: the number of steps leading up to the front door. I wished that it had been eight, or that they'd at least been a bit steeper. The four steps were going to make charging the door with the ram a little more difficult, but not that much more.

Stan called the police and gave them the news.

The dispatcher promised to get a first response vehicle to us within three minutes, and a fully-staffed riot van within fifteen. "Wankers," was Stan's uncompromising judgment. "What do they think the first response unit's going to achieve against— how many ED thugs are there?"

"Sixteen," Jim informed him, dolefully. "And some of the other people are taking hold of the battering-ram too. There's another crowd coming up the hill—must be the drinkers from the Crown and Bells. This is bad."

"The boozers don't count," said Stan. "They've just come to watch. Even the bastards who are grabbing a bit of the ram are just in it for the fun. The ram's not a bad thing, really—it's obviously theatrical, more symbolic than merely brutal. There's every chance that they're just putting on a show, and don't really intend to hurt anyone. Anyone see any guns or knives?"

"Nothing in plain view," Marjorie reported. "They've mostly got loose fitting combat-jackets on, though, and those stupid jeans with all the zip-pockets. My guess is that some of them will be carrying concealed handguns, but no Kalashnikovs or Uzis."

"Pity," Stan said, with a sigh. "If they were waving firearms around, even the Thames Valley Police would feel obliged to scramble a copter and an Armed Response Vehicle."

"Maybe you should just tell the cops they've got guns," Kevin suggested. "It's almost certainly true, as Marjorie says."

"Best not," Stan said. "If an ARV does turn up, and the ED boys think it incumbent on them to defend themselves, people could get hurt. If it's just a riot squad, the nutters will probably be content to keep their popguns in their pockets. Even mob violence has its regs."

The regs in question obviously permitted stone-throwing. As soon as the first tentative stone had hit the window, it turned into a shower, and the shower rapidly became a deluge. A lot of the missiles bounced off the bars or the windows, but three or four came through within a minute, spraying shards of glass across the floor before everyone had had time to take cover.

Then the battering ram hit the door for the first time, and Stan turned into Action Man, bellowing orders. He thought he was in charge—and to be honest, I was as glad as everyone else appeared to be that he did. As requested, I raced to station myself by his side. So did Jim Peel and the most able-bodied of the older males.

"Kev—you and Mike strip the sheets from my bunk and the spare, and try to fix them up over the windows to intercept the flying glass. Grab a broom each, and if anyone reaches through a broken window with a gun, knock it out of his hand. Nicky, Jim, grab that table and wedge it against the doors—then upend the other one, fold up the legs and lay it on of the first. The rest of you, fold up the chairs, and pile them on top—then put a couple of armchairs on top of the stack, for good measure. Quickly—once the barricade's formed, everybody get behind and brace yourselves. The longer we can prevent the door from breaking, the more chance there is that the riot squad will be able to nip this in the bud. You'll thank me for working you all so hard if we can keep them out."

"There are too many of them!" Jim said mournfully, glacing through the as-yet-unobscured window as he lumbered forward to help me with the first of the trestle-tables. "It's not just the ED—they're all joining in."

"No they're not!" Stan retorted. "And they won't, if we can just keep things under control. Work together—and *don't panic!*"

The battering ram hit the door again. It juddered, but didn't break. The tables and chairs were formed up into an inner barricade now, and a dozen of us put our weight behind it, with Jim in the center. Stan and I were positioned to either side of him, bracing ourselves for the third crash.

"Is Timmy with them?" Pearl asked, trying to peer out of the imperilled window to the left of the door while helping Kevin to secure the sheet from Stan's bunk.

"No," Marjorie reported. "He made himself scarce as soon as the ED appeared."

"That's good," said Pearl. "That's good." She didn't specify whether it was because she didn't want her loyal stalker getting hurt, or because she was simply glad that he hadn't joined in with the people who were coming to get her—and perhaps to lynch her—because she'd been labeled an angel of death by dodgy rumor-feeds.

The battering-ram hit the door for a third time. The door was beginning to splinter, and the barricade threatened to fly apart. "Hold it together!" Stan commanded—although it wasn't an order that could be easily obeyed. The rain of stones and other objects hitting the other wall of the building seemed to be very loud—but the whole point of it seemed to be to make a noise. As Stan said, it was theatrical rather than merely brutal. The ED were acting the part of besiegers storming a redoubt.

The theatricality, I knew, might turn out to be more dangerous than any acts of violence they eventually achieved. It would encourage the gawkers to join in, giving them a script for comprising an angry mob—and there were a hundred cameras of every sort jostling for a ringside position

"It's going out live on three high-profile news-feeds," Methuselah reported, from the mezzanine, as if to confirm my fears. "As soon as one of the networks starts putting it out, we'll have millions of eyes on us. The ED aren't even trying to stop the paparazzi taking pictures."

"Of course not," Stan said. "That's what they want. This is purely a publicity stunt."

As if to underline his claim, the telegraph pole smashed into the door for a third time. The rammers were building up a rhythm now.

As if to drown out the ominous thunder, Stand started shouting again. "Pearl! Get behind the counter in the kitchenette and *keep your head down*. Jim, if the door gives, go stand in the kitchenette doorway. Just lean on the jamb, as if you were passing the time of day, but *keep it blocked*. Marjorie, Alice—gather all the women in the store-room *now*, lock the door and *don't bloody argue*. Kevin, if the door gives, go put *Highway to Hell* on the blaster...."

"I don't...," I began.

"Shut up, Nicky—it's for my benefit, not theirs. Everybody else—and that includes you, Son—if the door breaks, get up to the mezzanine or into the corners of the room. Make yourselves as small as you possibly can, and *don't get involved*. I'll front it out. I know how to handle these fuckers, and the fewer targets they have ready to hand, the more chance there is of talking instead of brawling. They may be idiots, but they've got their headline now—with luck, they'll let the police clear them away, pretending all the while to be victims of establishment politics."

The battering ram hit the door again. We leaned into the impact as best we could, but the screws holding the door hinges were already coming away, and the battens were cracking from top to bottom. It was obvious that the door was going to break, and that the barricade made out of tables and chairs would be reduced soon afterwards to flying debris, no matter how hard we tried to hold it together and brace it with our own feeble strength. I couldn't see a thing through the doors, but I could easily imagine than there must be as many as forty people manning the battering-ram now, treating it as a bit of alcohol-fueled fun, not knowing or caring what would happen after the door caved in.

I could hear police sirens, and knew that the riot van could only be a couple of minutes away—provided that the streets were clear. I had an awful suspicion that they wouldn't be.

This is serious, I thought. I had to remind myself, because it all seemed so surreal. But I was quick to rebuild my morale as best I could: *But it's not the bloody Alamo. This is Merry England, not the Wild West.*

Then the battering ram hit the door again, and the hinges gave way. Once the wood split, the weight of the doors lent its own momentum to the shock of the impact. As soon as the battens began to fall, it was obvious that nothing behind the double door was going to put up any significant resistance, even though the sheer bulk of the secondary barricade stopped the battens from crashing down immediately. We all stepped back.

Every man who was still there did exactly what he had been told to do—except me. Kevin went to put *Highway to Hell* on the blaster. Jim went to stand in the doorway of the kitchenette. Some of the others clambered up to the crowded mezzanine; the rest moved back into the corners. I guess I just hadn't been doing rockmobility long enough to have got into the habit of following Stan's orders. I wasn't being insubordinate, let alone brave. I was just confused. I didn't know which corner to head for, or whether to join the queue for the stairs up to the mezzanine, so I just stayed where I was, hesitating.

Where I was happened to be a couple of paces behind Stan, and a couple to his left, relative to the broken door.

I was still there when the battens were unceremoniously shoved aside and the monsters surged through.

The remains of secondary barricade were still in their way, but they flung it aside with the casual ease that monsters always manifest, when something is getting between them and their intended prey. None of the flying debris reached as far as me, and Stan only had to swat away one skidding chair, but any faint hope we might have had that the ED thugs would spend four or five minutes stumbling and tripping over like the Keystone Cops on acid went right out of the broken windows.

In fact, presumably following a carefully-prepared script, more than half of the thirty amply-booted brutes who'd brought the ram continued to hang on to it as they drew it back into the street, turning it through ninety degrees so that they could use it as a wall against the riot police, who still hadn't contrived to get the van up the hill past the boozers from the Crown and Bells. More than half of the rest were holding a non-violent but conscientiously-obstructive discussion with the members of the police first-response team.

Thanks to the fact that the huge doorway was now wide open, I could see the distant riot-van and the ongoing discussion quite clearly—and a whole lot more. Suddenly, the deafening thunder of *Highway to Hell* didn't seem so inappropriate—and it didn't seen ironic at all. The monsters didn't seem in the least surprised or alarmed by it. It was probably their kind of music—but Stan really did seem to be drawing strength from it, standing tall and firm like a true knight.

All the world really is a stage, and all the people in it merely players, but it seemed to me that a good two-thirds of the hundred-and-fifty-strong crowd now gathered outside hardly even qualified as spear-carriers. They were just swarming extras, intent on raising the arms in which they were holding their phones or dedicated cameras to get a better view. Their *avant garde* was crowding the steps of the Hall, but making no effort to rush in. I only hoped that when the riot cops eventually got past the telegraph-pole, they'd be able to force a way through in order to come to our aid, however belatedly.

Only four of the ED thugs actually crossed the threshold, although three more remained on the steps, as if to hold back the crowd. Given that they probably had paid employment as night-club bouncers, I figured that they were probably experienced men who knew what they were doing and could cope with the task—but anybody can be wrong.

One of the four who'd made an entrance stepped forward to confront Stan—who was, as he'd promised, simply waiting there to "front it out". Unsurprisingly, the monster who stepped forward was the biggest of the four—big enough to make Jim look like a modest individual, let alone Stan.

The giant was wearing the standard khaki waistcoat and trousers, both garment bristling with oddly-shaped and bulging pockets, but unlike his followers he wasn't wearing a T-shirt. His chest was bare, evidently to display his pride in his very extensive tattoos. He had a lot of them, including the obligatory flags of St. George, swastikas, daggers and dragons, but pride of place on his vast clean-shaven chest as a golden eagle with its wings outspread, perched on a cartouche bearing the motto: *Pro Patria Mori*.

I was tempted to ask him what kind of Englishman would walk around with a Latin motto sprawled across his navel, but I didn't dare, Stan wouldn't have approved.

"Where's the girl?" demanded the patriot. "We've come for the angel of death. Hand her over, and nobody will get hurt."

Stan didn't bother to ask what they intended to do with Pearl if they got their grubby hands on her, or even to compliment his adversary on what was probably the longest speech he'd ever made in his life. Instead—and I have to admit that he took me completely by surprise, although I probably should have been expecting it—he simply reached up to the collar of his black T-shirt with both hands, and literally ripped it from top to bottom, following the line of the sternum.

Then he pulled the torn halves apart and said: "There's no need for this, Brother." Maybe the appeal to brotherhood would have sounded more convincing if Kevin hadn't followed Stan's instructions and put *Highway to Hell* on the blaster, but maybe not. The words were, after all, *supposed* to be ironic.

I couldn't resist taking two steps forward, just to see what it was that Stan had tattooed on his chest—the broad chest that had always been covered by a black T-shirt during the fortnight I'd known him. That movement brought me to stand right beside him, almost shoulder-to-shoulder with him—a side-effect I hadn't even considered, let alone planned.

As if in reflexive response, the ED Goliath's three companions each took a diagonal step forward, in order to wind up virtually shoulder-to-shoulder with the monster-in-chief and one another.

More flying buttresses, I could help thinking.

Stan didn't tell me off for not obeying orders, but he certainly didn't seem glad to see me there when he risked a brief sideways glance.

The tattoo on his chest was a phoenix. The cartouche on which it was perched bore the motto: *England Will Rise Again*. It was a very impressive tattoo. The eagle, big and ferocious as it was, had something of the air of an old sepia photograph about it, by virtue of its suntanned background. Stan's skin was polished ivory, delicately striped with blue veins. The accidentally-prophetic phoenix and the fire of its miraculous rebirth stood out beautifully, all their artificial colors flamboyantly ablaze. I only hoped that the cameras in the doorway could capture the full effect.

The reason that Stanley Blake was so convinced that he "knew how to handle these fuckers," I belatedly realized, was that he had been one of them. *Had been* being the operative words. Becoming a zombie changes people.

It also, unfortunately, means that even your very best comedy moves fall flat.

Stan knew perfectly well that what he'd just done was absurd. He knew that it was beyond melodrama, way out in the realm of the ludicrous. I honestly believe that he expected it to raise a laugh, or at least a chuckle. He had never expected for an instant that his erstwhile colleague was going to respond to the word "Brother" by falling into his arms and declaring that the war was over—but he had expected a better and kinder pause than he actually got. He had expected, at least, a twinge of amusement, a recognition of the irony of fate.

Instead, the ED Goliath was actually spooked. He didn't know what to do, or say. His prepared script hadn't included any such possibility. Although there was no need, he panicked, and lost his rag.

He didn't have a real actor's talent for improvisation. His own reflexes were the monster variety. Had he had time to think about it, and half a brain to think about it with, he probably wouldn't have done what he did, but the sight of the phoenix was like a trigger to his feral instincts. In response to Stan's challenge, even though it wasn't really a challenge at all, the marauding monster reached into one of his multitudinous pockets and pulled out a handgun.

CHAPTER THIRTEEN

If ever they make a movie of my memoirs, for which I shall naturally be asked to write the script, everything will be done on a much more lavish scale. Instead of being crammed so tightly against its neighboring buildings that there was no alleyway to the back yard, the hall where the heroic afterliving are besieged will be free-standing, and surrounded, and it will have the words *Kingdom Hall* on its lintel instead of *Salvation Army*, which is just as plausible, given that Jehovah's Witnesses have built similar meeting-places and have also had to sell off many of them as their numbers have declined. At any rate, that legend seems more appropriate to me, for symbolic purposes.

The extras will be assaulting the Hall from every side, smashing shuttered windows and reaching inside with avid arms, trying to stab or grab anything within. Most of the extras will be computer-generated, of course, so there won't just be hundreds of them but thousands: a veritable rabid horde rather than a mere drunken mob. And the siege will last for at least half an hour, rather than a lousy few minutes—not exactly the Alamo, but not your average inner-city street-brawl either. Epic, after its fashion.

I'll insist that the tattoos be faithfully reproduced, and the stature of the Goliath really won't need any exaggeration. He can't have that gun, though, because, to be perfectly honest, the gun was entirely inappropriate to the situation. I'll give him a samurai sword instead—a sword with which he intends to subject poor Pearl, our inexpressively lovely damsel in distress, to a public beheading right there and then, to demonstrate that England's Finest can match any jihadists in the world, blow for blow, when it comes to crass bloodthirstiness.

I think I'll arm the actor playing me with a brass candlestick, so that he can engage the samurai sword in a fencing-match. I know there aren't many brass candlesticks around nowadays, but it's not entirely implausible that we might have a supply of candles in the Hall and apparatus for their distribution, not so much because of our distaste for brighter light but because of the increasing frequency of "rationed power cuts."

Anyway, you can get away with anything in a movie, as long as it's violent and you keep up the narrative flow. Fencing matches are always okay—even fencing matches between a villain armed with a samurai sword and a hero with a brass candlestick. Never mind the thinking, and forget the explanations, *just get on with the bloody story....*

In a movie, you have to do a lot with the few words you have, especially the title. My movie will, inevitably, be called *Night of the Living*—not just because it's about a horde of stupid malevolent drunks trying to break into a besieged building *at night* in order to slaughter a hapless flock of innocents who only want to get on with their afterlives in peace, but because the whole of the action will be symbolic. Because, you see, that microcosmic scene really will capture the very essence of world's inevitable fate: of the impending night of the living, and the dawn of the risen dead. The whole point of the scene is that, even though the living far outnumber the afterliving, and are far nastier, the afterliving are going to withstand their assault. They're going to pull through. They're going to survive.

And simply by surviving, they're planting a symbolic signpost to the future. The future, that signpost says—not in so many words, because this is a movie, and you can't interrupt the action just to make people think, but tacitly—is ours. Maybe not today, and maybe not tomorrow, but one day, we'll be running the show.

We'll be running the show because we deserve to run it, and

because, after all, somebody has to, and we couldn't possibly make a worse job of it than the living, even if we *are* only human.

That's what the movie is all about, you see. It's about arguing, however ludicrous it might seem in terms of the calculus of probability, that the candlestick really is mightier than the sword, because it's capable, given a candle, of bearing light, and isn't just a dedicated device designed to slice and dice human flesh.

The movie is about the insistence that everything will work out in the end, that Utopia is not only conceivable, but achievable, if only the right million-to-one shot falls out of the chaos of possibility. That's a lot easier to contrive, of course, if you have a single scriptwriter with his heart in the right place than a committee of the whole world, but we mustn't forget that, living and afterliving alike, we really do have the power to remake our world. We're the ones who do things, the ones that make things happen.

It could be a great movie.

It won't be anything much like the original book, of course, because the original book is an autobiography, and has to be true to afterlife, but movies never are.

* * * * * * *

The gun that Goliath pulled out was only a small gun—it had to be, in order to have fitted into his pocket, but it was still a gun, and it rewrote the script for the entire melodrama within the twinkling of an eye.

For one thing, it licensed the police to scramble a helicopter and an Armed Response Vehicle, without having to be called and asked—but that wasn't really relevant to Stan and me, because we knew full well that whatever was going to happen now was going to play out a lot faster than the measured power-ballet that the cops were choreographing, and a lot faster than anyone had intended or hoped.

Stan actually began to say: "There's no need…," but he didn't even have time to finish the futile sentence.

"Traitor!" spat the man with the eagle tattoo, who presumably didn't know that the first half of his chosen motto was *Dulce et Decorum Est*. There wasn't an atom of sweetness or decorousness about him—and he didn't look as if he had the slightest intention of dying for his fatherland.

But he didn't shoot right away. However bad he was at improvisation, he knew that this was still supposed to be a play, still a publicity stunt, still a parade of apparent strength and resolution, for the benefit of the cameras. He knew that it wasn't supposed to turn into a massacre. He knew that there was no need…but now that his inner scriptwriter had lost the plot, his instincts were running riot.

Anything could happen.

The words to *Highway to Hell* faded away, leaving silence. It's not a very long song.

Stan decided to change tack. He was a much better improviser than Goliath. "Go ahead, then, Brother," he said, calmly and quietly. "Shoot me. I'm already dead. The only person you can hurt is yourself."

It was, I suppose, an obvious gambit. Too obvious, perhaps.

Pearl suddenly shoved her way past Jim Peel—improbable as that sounds—and stood out in the open, about fifteen feet behind us.

"Stan isn't the one you want," she said. "I'm your angel of death. Let these two alone and I'll go with you. There's nothing you can do to me that hasn't been done already."

I assumed that she was just playing for time, and that her inner scriptwriter was simply desperate. Remarkably, though, it provoked a riposte that actually scored a point for us.

"You might think you've been raped before, Honey," the monster said—even the ED research their targets on the internet—"but you ain't felt nothing yet."

It was probably the most stupid thing he could possibly have said, precisely because it reflected his true feelings and his true identity. I'd already cast him as a monster, of course, be the whole point of his being there, and the whole point of his entire pathetic existence, from his own viewpoint, was to pose as one of England's Defenders. Threatening to rape a damsel in distress—even a zombie damsel in distress—made him the Dragon, not St. George, Goliath, not David, a shambling, ghoulish wreck of a human being, not a hero.

As soon as he'd said it, he realized that it had been a silly mistake. Everybody watches TV, even if they favor shows that are much more violent and slightly more melodramatic than *Resurrection Ward*, and don't have their hearts in the right place.

Still improvising, the giant rotated his right arm through thirty degrees or so, and dropped it by a few inches, so that the gun was pointing straight at my forehead.

"I can blow his fucking brains out," he observed, with uncomfortable accuracy. "He won't be coming back from the dead again then, will he? None of you will, if we do the job right." Personally, I thought, was a low blow. It was also an invitation to his three flying buttresses to draw their own guns—which they did.

Now, I thought, *things have really turned ugly. Now, it really is going to be a massacre. It* is *the Alamo, after all.*

All Stan had to come back with, unfortunately, was: "Leave the boy out of it. He has nothing to do with this."

"He walked the zombie nurse home last night," the well-informed ED thug remarked, "and that green bitch Claridge too."

It suddenly occurred to me, belatedly, that Mum and Dad would be watching the show—and Kirsten too. I figured that I owed it to the at least to put in a line of my own. They wouldn't have wanted me to look like the kind of idiot who got stick with a non-speaking role. If I was going down, I had to go down as Davy Crockett, not an extra.

"I have everything to do with this," I said looking Goliath straight in the eye. "And I have *you* to thank for that, don't I? I was in the Oracle when *your* idiot bomber blew himself to bloody shreds. Obviously, you didn't do that personally, but I'm sure you'd be glad to accept your share of the responsibility. I presume that it was some other expert rapist who drove poor Pearl to suicide, but you've just boasted about your willingness to do the same, and worse, so the fact that we're here, and all that we are, really is *your* doing, isn't it? Congratulations on a world well made."

I was just playing for time. I wasn't trying particularly hard to make him look bad, and I wasn't really trying to goad him… well, maybe just a little bit. I still couldn't quite believe that he was going to blow my brains while he was live on broadcast news. If he'd been that kind of martyr, I figured, it *would* have been him in the Oracle with a semtex vest and a battery-powered detonator.

As things turned out, though, I never got to find out whether or not he would have shot me, because we were interrupted.

The doormen, even though there were three of them, turned out to be absolute crap at their job, perhaps because their attention was focused exclusively on the riot police. Not that it's easy to be brave and purposeful if someone is waving a Kalashnikov in your face—especially someone who looks plenty crazy enough to use it.

Actually, I can barely tell a Kalashnikov from a blunderbuss. Maybe it was an Armalite, or some brand of gun that I'd never even heard of. All I know for sure is that the weapon that was being waved—and I do mean *waved*—by the crazy person who came in through the broken doorway, the entire crowd outside having hurriedly made way for him, was *some* kind of rifle.

The crazy person in question was about five foot three and slightly-built. He wasn't a day over nineteen. It was Pearl's stalker, Timmy. He hadn't made himself scarce at all when the ED turned up. He'd gone to fetch his gun from wherever he'd parked his silly little car.

I was flabbergasted to discover that he had a gun. So was Goliath.

I couldn't imagine for a moment that he actually meant to fire it, or that he could possibly hit what he was aiming at if he did. Neither could Goliath.

Anybody can be wrong.

"Leave her alone!" Timmy said—or, rather, screeched. "Just get the hell out of here and leave her alone."

"Take that gun off him before he hurts himself," the man with the eagle tattoo said to one of his evil henchmen.

The henchman in question stepped forward, without an instant's hesitation.

Suddenly, the rifle wasn't waving any longer, Suddenly, it was perfectly steady, braced against Timmy's shoulder. Suddenly, the henchman's right knee exploded, and he collapsed like a ton of bricks, dropping his own pathetic handgun.

It's surprising how quickly you can change your mind, under the right stimulus. I never even considered the possibility that the shot had gone wild. I knew that Timmy had hit exactly what he had been aiming for. And I *knew*, when he swung the barrel round to point it at Goliath, who was still in the process of turning round to face the new monster-slayer on the block, that if he fired again, Timmy would hit exactly what he was aiming at. He was only ten feet away, and I had the advantage of having heard Pearl reveal that his beloved mother was a member of the "County Set." Although that didn't necessarily mean that Timmy's Dad was heavily into hunting and shooting, it certainly didn't imply that he wasn't. And what self-respecting member of the Berkshire Hunt wouldn't have taught his little boy to shoot, especially if the kid was a bit of a runt?

The monster with the eagle tattoo, of course, had the disadvantage of not having heard that. Unlike me, he wasn't sure that Timmy's first shot hadn't gone astray. He presumably knew the law—most people who carry guns know at least a little of it—and was well aware that if he shot Timmy now, he'd be able to plead self-defence. Perhaps he took that as a licence to kill. At any rate, he aimed his own pathetic little popgun at Timmy's weedy chest.

That particular law, however, cuts both ways. Timmy could have blown Goliath's brains out then, and gotten away with it. He didn't. Instead, he altered his stance ever so slightly and shot

Goliath in the knee, exactly as he had done to the henchman.

Goliath went down like a second ton of bricks, but he didn't let go of his gun. He wasn't dead, and he was too big and stupid even to lose consciousness—and he still had hold of his gun.

By this time, the monster's other two evil henchmen were exercising their own stupidity by wondering whether might be a good time to use their own weapons. It wasn't, but only one of them had presence of mind enough to figure that out, check the gesture, drop his weapon and raise his arms above his head instead.

The other had no presence of mind at all, and entirely the wrong instincts. As soon as he raised the hand clutching the pistol, as if to aim, Timmy shot him in the knee too.

I certainly wouldn't have wanted to be a grouse on his father's favorite Highland moor, or a crow on the family farm.

In the street behind the rapt audience I saw a police Armed Response Vehicle pull up in the street. Armored men with rifles of their own started to pile out. It must have been lurking close at hand, just in case. The one thought in my mind was: *For God's sake don't shoot Timmy—not until he's finished, at least.*

But Timmy *had* finished, absurd as that seemed. As if in super-slo-mo, I watched the stricken monster with the eagle tattoo raise his own pistol, aiming straight at Timmy's valiant heart.

I knew, without a shadow of a doubt, that Timmy still had time to bring the rifle round again, take expert aim, and blow the monster's stupid brains out for him.

But that wasn't what Timmy did. He didn't even shoot out the other knee.

Instead, he raised his own arms in the air, as if mimicking the evil henchman's gesture of surrender. For a split second, I actually thought that his was a gesture of surrender too—and so, in all probability, did the man with the eagle tattoo.

Goliath fired anyway. He had nothing on his mind now but vengeance. He wasn't thinking about destroying brains any longer, though; he just fired at the biggest part of what wasn't all that big a target.

It was a fine shot, in the circumstances, although it was never going to win England's Defenders any points in what was now one of the greatest PR cock-ups of the twenty-first century.

Timmy the Martyr, hastening to his Resurrection and his mystical union with his beloved Pearl, took the bullet full in the chest. It knocked him backwards like a rag doll. Blood fountained from his torn arteries.

Goliath was already pulling the gun around, knowing now that that any self-defence plea he might have copped before had gone right out of the window. He wasn't trying bring it to bear on me, the poor innocent bystander, but on Stanley Blake the traitor—who might, I suppose, have taken action himself, but might equally well have realized that Timmy had just set the bar for looking good that little bit higher, and figured that he could take a bullet in the chest as well as any living poseur.

It didn't matter. I couldn't have hit a barn door with a rifle-shot to save my afterlife, but I knew how to volley a soccer ball. I kicked the hand that was holding Goliath's gun harder than I'd ever kicked a football in an entire career of Sunday mornings.

Maybe the monster could have held on, but the effort would probably have snapped his trigger-finger, and the shot released in consequence could have gone anywhere—except for Stan's phoenix-tattooed torso. In fact, the crippled thug let go, and his pathetic little popgun soared high over Timmy's stricken body and into the eager crowd still packed into the gaping doorway.

Then I leapt over the moaning, spitting, bleeding monstrosity and reached Timmy with what felt like a single bound, although it must have been at least three strides. I left Stan way behind—without *Highway to Hell* to inspire him, the poor lamb was quite at a loss, although the phoenix on his chest still looked magnificent, and its symbolic value hadn't diminished in the slightest.

Timmy wasn't quite dead yet, but there was nothing to be done that could possibly have prolonged his life for more than a few seconds more. He was trying to say something. It was probably just Pearl's name, but he might have had something more elaborate prepared.

I had to speak for him—there was no one else in position, although Pearl was coming as fast as she could. I really wished that I'd had the opportunity to prepare something, but I had to go with the flow and let my instincts take over. There was no time for thinking, let alone for explanations. It just happened.

It was probably the hammiest line I could possibly have come up with, but it wasn't inappropriate, in the circumstances. I just looked up into all the phones and cameras that were jostling for position in the doorway, completely blocking the path of the armed police, then nodded down at Timmy's dead but hopefully resurrectable body, and said: "*That* is a True Briton, and a true Knight of the Living Dead. In a couple of weeks' time, we'll be throwing him one *hell* of a party."

Then the police broke through and started pouring in like a great blue cataract. There was nothing left for them to do but pick up the pieces, but I expect that's the way they like it.

While Pearl knelt down beside Timmy, to make sure that he was still fit for a long and prosperous afterlife, I turned back to the fallen monster, and gave him a great big beaming smile.

"Don't worry, my darling boy," I said to him. "She'll probably be your nurse too, once she's off suspension. You'll get the very best of her attention—she's an authentic angel of mercy. The last thing she'll want is to let you die."

I didn't get a laugh, though. That's the only downside to afterlife: everybody around you loses their sense of humor.

EPILOGUE

As soon as I had a spare moment, I did my duty and phoned home, while standing in a pool of blood that wasn't mine. There must have been quite a scramble to get to the landline receiver, and Dad's hard to defeat when he wants to say "I told you so," but it was only fair that Kirsten beat him to it. What Dad wanted to remind me that he'd told me was that I should have stayed at home instead of going into the Center, but Kirsten had been right to back me up when I said that I had to.

"Hi, Kirsty," I said. "Just phoning to let you know that I'm okay."

"We know," she said. "We've been watching TV."

"How did I come across, on a scale of one to ten? In terms of heroism, I mean."

"In terms of heroism, maybe four; in terms of stupidity, at least eight." She always had been a harsh marker. No man is a hero to his little sister, no matter how hard he tries.

"Well," I said, "I survived."

There was no polite answer to that. "When I said you had to be there," she told me, "I didn't mean that you had to be in the middle of it. I didn't mean that you had to stick your head in the lion's mouth."

"He wasn't a lion," I said, "he was a monster. And I reckon that if you're going to be somewhere at all, you might as well be right in the middle. Otherwise, you're just settling for being a spear-carrier, or some mug taking murky and jerky video pictures with a mobile phone."

"Are you coming home now?" she asked.

"Actually, no," I said. "The action might be over but the play goes on. We still need to show solidarity. We can't stay here, of course—the place is a hell of a mess as well as a multiple crime-scene, so we're all going to march *en masse*, as if in triumph, to the hostel in South Street. There aren't enough rooms there for us to have one each, but we'll cope, when the party finally winds down."

"Don't drink too much," she said, probably repeating an instruction from Mum.

"Zombies never do," I assured her.

"And don't do anything I wouldn't do."

"There's no polite answer to that."

"And *be careful*. You might have survived this round, but things won't be any different tomorrow."

"Yes they will," I said. "Not much different, perhaps, in purely practical terms, or even in the way that people look at us when they see us in the supermarket, or kicking a ball around in a field—but trust me, a difference has been made."

"You are coming home eventually? You're not going to move into the hostel permanently?"

"No room—and there'll be other zombies coming through who'll need accommodation more than I will. Something tells me that Timmy's County Set parents might take a dim view of what he just did for love of his zombie maid. I'll be back some time tomorrow to begin catching up on my retraining course. Afterlife goes on, and there'll always be a bureaucratic game to play. I'm going to apply for a job at the BBC, though—got to cash in on my celebrity while it's still hot."

"What as? Please don't say stand-up comedian."

"Don't be silly—this is serious. As a presenter and commentator. It's about time we had an afterlife current affairs show. We can't let *Resurrection Ward* shape our image forever."

"Good luck with that," she said.

"Thanks," I replied, with perfect sincerity.

* * * * * * *

Pearl came over as soon as she saw that I was no longer on the phone.

"It was really stupid of you to get stuck in the crossfire zone like that," she said, "but thanks."

"I had a premonition that it might all go wrong if I wasn't there to do my humble bit," I said, before switching my honesty back on to say: "but I'm not the one you have to thank. Assuming that you're back on duty when he comes out of pupation, thank him for me too, will you."

"I *told* you he was harmless," she said—and smiled.

"You did," I agreed. "I suppose I've lost my chance now—there's no way I can ever compete with your knight in shining armor."

"His armor wasn't shining," she pointed out, accurately. "Anyway, you've already got a girl-friend. What was her name again?"

"Helena," I said. "Her name *is* Helena."

Bang on cue, my new phone rang—and when I looked down at the screen….

"It's her," I said.

For a split second, Pearl seemed sceptical, but then she capitulated with the whim of fate.

"Good luck with that," she said, and turned away.

I retreated into a distant corner, where there was hardly any blood on the floor.

"Hi," I said, thinking that more than one syllable might be dangerous as well as difficult.

"Are you okay?" Helena asked.

"You know I am," I told her. "You've been watching the TV."

"I still am," she said. "I just wanted to make sure."

"And what if I weren't?"

"Then I'd be sad. I still care, you know. In fact, I'm still in love, but…."

"With the living me," I finished for her. "The man I used to be."

"Yes. I'm glad you understand."

I did—or thought I did. I thought I could explain it now, at least to myself. "It's hard for me," I told her. "You haven't changed, you see. You're still the person the living me was in love with…and inside, I still feel the same."

"I know," she said. "I'm sorry."

"So am I—but I do understand. I have a lot to be grateful for. My old self was a lazy sod, who really didn't appreciate the life he had. He just drifted through it, making wisecracks, without any sense of direction or purpose…except in regard to you. Thanks to you, he knew what it was to love someone. He knew what it as to have a reason for living. That was infinitely precious to him, although he never quite realized it at the time. It's infinitely previous to me too, and I do realize it. Thanks to you, I wasn't just alive—I had *a life*. And because I had a life, my afterlife is better by far than what it might have been. I could have died as Peter Pan, never having grown up, but thanks to you, my afterlife really will be an awfully big adventure, built on a sound foundation."

"That's bullshit," she said, cruelly. "I was only a part of your life. You had your parents, your sister, your e-reader, your football…." She didn't bother to mention my job; there was no need to go to absurd lengths.

"That's all true," I said, "but you were the center, the rest was just the periphery. You were the fulcrum, the hub, the…sorry, I've run out of synonyms."

"Axis," she suggested. "Pivot. Focal point. Primary sex-object." She was a primary school teacher. She was good at synonym-hunting, although she sometimes slipped in a dud.

"Yes," I said. "All of that."

"You won't spin out of control for long, Nicky. As I said, I'm sorry. But as I said, I just can't. I did want to make sure that you're okay, though. Be careful. Be safe—and when you can, be happy."

"You too," I said.

"I will," she promised—and I tried not to take it too hard.

****

This time, it was Stan and Methuelah who had been hovering, waiting for me to get off the phone. He was still bare-chested.

"Thanks, Mate," Stan said. "Good kick."

"You're welcome," I told him. "Nice phoenix."

"It looks better on me now than it did in life," he agreed. "Maybe I had a premonition."

"Maybe you did," I agreed. "Sorry I didn't follow orders."

"Maybe you had a premonition too," he suggested generously. "Anyway, I'm not really in charge, not officially—it's just that I'm such a loudmouth that everybody thinks I am."

"They trust your judgment," I told him. "Even about rock-mobility."

He nodded his head, sagely. "They know it's good for them," he agreed. "But you and me, we really *enjoy* it, don't we?"

"We do," I confirmed.

Methuselah took advantage of the pause that followed to say: "You really didn't have to do that. The police would have sorted it out." That's the ultimate function of a Wise Old Man: to be wise after every event.

"But you're glad we did, aren't you?" I said.

He didn't have to answer that.

"You do realize," Stan said, after a long look around the Hall, "that we're going to have to fix this place up ourselves, don't you?" he said. "The Council will take forever if we leave it to them. It's going to mean a lot of hard work—and I'm relying on you to do more than your fair share, Nicky, with your being so young and fit."

"I'm ready if you are," I assured him. "I don't think any of us will be found wanting."

"No," said Methuselah. "They'll all do their bit."

"We need to look at it as a golden opportunity, though, rather than a bitter necessity," I told them. "If we put some effort into it, we could really do something with the place—make it more of a home from home. We'll need someone with a good eye for interior decoration, mind. Somehow, Stan, I suspect that your tastes and mine might be reckoned a trifle elementary by the truly sophisticated."

He grinned. "Mine, anyway," he said. "Old headbanger, me. Might take me quite a while to grow out of it. You're a man of taste, though. I can see that."

"Not when it comes to wallpaper and soft furnishings," I said. "Alice is probably your best bet for that sort of thing. Something tells me that Marjorie isn't much into frippery."

Stan grinned again. "We'll be setting off for the hostel in a few minutes," he told me. "The cops are just about ready to let us go—they want the place to themselves for a while, although I can't see that there's much for forensics to do—they've got the whole bloody thing on a hundred different tapes."

"It's procedure," I said. "We all have our scripts to follow. Lucky that ours is the one with the happy ending, isn't it?"

"Right," he said, a trifle dubiously. I must have looked surprised at his lack of enthusiasm, because he glanced at my phone expressively. Maybe he had overheard a few things, or maybe he had just been tracking my facial expressions.

"Maybe not entirely happy, in conventional terms," I admitted, "but we're zombies—we don't exist in conventional terms. We're still busy reinventing ourselves, and figuring out our own recipes for happiness…but that, in itself, is the happiest of all possible endings, for the time being, don't you think?"

"Amen to that," said the Wise Old Man

"Old headbanger, me," Stan reminded me. "Haven't a clue what you're talking about, Mate." But he didn't mean it. He knew.

* * * * * * *

"Limelight-hogging little creep!" Marjorie muttered, when I fell into step with her as we all set off on the triumphal march from the former Salvation Army Hall to the former Bail Hostel. "I was watching you, you know, on my phone. We all were, huddled in that bloody cupboard. Why on earth did I let Stan order me away like that? I should have been out there, shouting the odds. At least Methuselah was up on the balcony, cheering you on. Stan's got a bloody cheek, taking it for granted that the poor weak women needed to be shielded from the nasty men."

"He was in charge," I reminded her. "Somebody had to be. You can't really blame him for his chivalrous instincts. He knew that it didn't matter if his brains got blown out—or mine, for that matter—but he had to make sure that you were safe. You're our propagandist-in-chief, the one person whose life we had to preserve at all costs, in order to tell our story and make our case."

"Flattery," she said, with a sigh, "will get you almost anywhere. Pity there's nowhere you want to go."

"I don't know about that," I told her. "I rather thought that once we get to South Street, you might invite me up for a cup of coffee."

She looked at me long and hard, her pink eyes blinking even in the feeble glare of the street-lights.

"Am I misunderstanding you?" she asked, dubiously.

"I don't think so," I told her.

"I thought you had a girl-friend."

"Not any more. Haven't had for quite some while—I just needed time to get used to the idea. Methuselah was dead right about the logic of the situation, but you know how hard it is to take good advice."

"I'm fifty-two, you know, Nicky," she observed, after a pause. "Almost twice your age."

"No you're not. You're at the very beginning of your afterlife, just like me. Old prejudices no longer count, and we need to shed them as soon as it's comfortable to do so. Everything is in front of us, and we have no idea, as yet, where true happiness is to be found."

"Come off it," she said. "You're as horny as hell because

you just narrowly escaped getting your brains blown out and valiantly kicked a madman's gun into touch, flooding your system with adrenalin—and you're desperate, because Pearl won't play."

"You have the most romantic way of putting things," I told her.

She laughed. She actually laughed—probably with mild self-satisfied delight rather than actual humor, but I wasn't fussy.

"I hope you won't regret it in the morning," she said, sincerely.

"I won't," I told her. "This is one of those nights—the first in my afterlife, and maybe my whole existence—when there's no longer any possibility of regret. I hope it won't be the last. There's a fair to middling chance, don't you think?"

"What self-respecting zombie could ask for anything more?" she countered, finally getting into the swing of the kind of wittily relaxed conversation that people with a lot in common ought to have.

And we marched on, into the coolly welcoming night.

ABOUT THE AUTHOR

Brian Stableford was born in Yorkshire in 1948. He taught at the University of Reading for several years, but is now a full-time writer. He has written many science-fiction and fantasy novels, including *The Empire of Fear*, *The Werewolves of London*, *Year Zero*, *The Curse of the Coral Bride*, *The Stones of Camelot*, and *Prelude to Eternity*. Collections of his short stories include a long series of *Tales of the Biotech Revolution*, and such idiosyncratic items as *Sheena and Other Gothic Tales* and *The Innsmouth Heritage and Other Sequels*. He has written numerous nonfiction books, including *Scientific Romance in Britain, 1890-1950*; *Glorious Perversity: The Decline and Fall of Literary Decadence*; *Science Fact and Science Fiction: An Encyclopedia*; and *The Devil's Party: A Brief History of Satanic Abuse*. He has contributed hundreds of biographical and critical articles to reference books, and has also translated numerous novels from the French language, including books by Paul Féval, Albert Robida, Maurice Renard, and J. H. Rosny the Elder.